All Kinds of CRAZY

Billie Dureyea Shell

Dedication

This Book is dedicated to Shriners Children Hospital these people help kids and make nothing for it it's time for us to invest in our future and the children are the future so 20% of the sells of this book will be donated to SHRINERS CHILDREN HOSPITAL

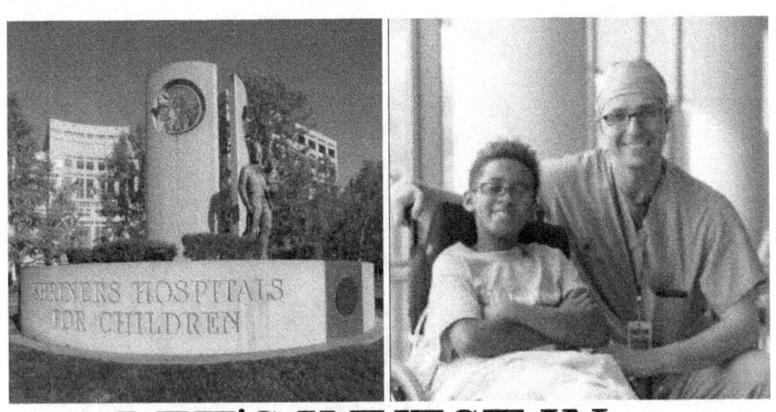

LET'S INVEST IN OUR FUTURE

ACKNOWLEDGEMENT

What's up y'all first and foremost I want to thank all my readers for buying the books that I've been putting out and supporting this journey that I'm going on writing. You guys have really made this writing shit something that I love to do the more you read it the more I write it without y'all putting these books out wouldn't even be worth it so I thank y'all and I love you all 2022 is here so let's get it......... To my Lord and Savior Jesus Christ thank you for blessing me with this talent and these skills I love you more than words could ever say you died on the cross for me and I know I wasn't worthy of it, so every day I'm going to try to prove to you that it wasn't in vain. To my mother, Mom I love you more than words could ever say we've been through the storm in the rain and we still here he was the first woman to ever have my back and I will always love you for that you know there's nothing that I won't do for you. And there's not enough money in the world to pay you back for all the shit I sent you through but I hope it was the things I am doing for you now I'm showing you how much you will appreciate it you always be my number one girl I love you Mama. To my little sister Glenda I miss you and I love you, you know I got your back no matter what and no matter what we go through I got to never change. To my beautiful wife and the love of my life Shatoya I never thought and I could find somebody that I would love just as much as I love myself yet a lot more everything that I have is yours and my heart belongs to you you always tell me that I'm the best part of you or little do you know you're the best part of me you get on my nerves and sometime I wonder is that your job. I love you for now forever and for always 1437. Call my kids and it's a lot of y'all so let's start in age order:

Jazmine, Ant'Juan, Devon, David, little Dureyea, Dillon, Alura, Avi, Cameron, Premiere, Shanice, and Anthony I love all of y'all you guys are the reason I smile. To my grandchildren Jordan, little Devon, and little Roman I love each one of y'all to Uncle Woody thank you for all you done in helping me to become a man you will always be my favorite uncle and a person I turned to for advice when this world get too hectic for me. To my cousin Zane R.I.P nigga I miss you more than words could ever express but just know that I'm down here holding it down and taking care of business and I promise you you'll never be forgotten. Call my nieces and nephews I love you all. To my big brother Lawrence thank you for all that you've done for me and showing me how to get it to my even older brother Fred you maybe you crazy but I still love you to my little cousin Cella you know I got you when you need me and I love you we are the fuck we got and we all fuck we need. To My uncle Woody only son R.I.P you messed and we love you and you won't be forgotten. To everybody else I didn't mention it ain't that I forgot you you just you just wasn't worth mentioning to all my dark side niggas you already know what it is keep doing what you're doing. Oh yeah a few shots cuz I don't want these people to think I'm saying fuck them Margo love you little sister Sade Love You Selena love you Shay Shay love you little Brandon and Lil Brian love y'all auntie Chris love you shit I think that's about it now enough of all this mushy stuff let's get to this book I hope you all enjoy reading as much as I enjoyed writing Happy New Year it's 2022 stay safe keep your mess on and let's get this money .....

Author Billie Dureyea Shell

PROLOGUE

Beads of sweat began to form on my forehead as I chased Moneca's husband around the room. He had a look of pure fear on his face as he ran from one side of the room to the other. I wanted to kill him. He attempted to slow me down by knocking down one of the chairs that sat in the office, but I quickly leaped over it and gripped the tail end of his shirt in my hand. I leaped onto his back and held on as he then began to spin around. "Ocean! Ocean!" I could hear someone calling for me to stop my attack, but at that moment, blinded by rage, I didn't care; I wanted blood. I began beating him on the top of his head as I then yelled, "I hate you! Die! Just die!" I was trying to pry my legs from around him while dodging my fists. He began to ram us both into the wall in hopes of making me fall, but I wanted him to suffer. I was relentless. I could feel someone trying to pull me off of him, but with the anger I was feeling inside, I wasn't letting up. He was the reason for all my suffering; for all my pain. After a few more tugging on my back, Dr. Green was finally able to pull me off and we both tumbled to the ground. I started swinging and yelling trying to get up and go after him again. Moneca's husband stood to his feet and raced to the other side of the room. His chest heaved up and down as he stared at me with fear in his eyes. "You have got to calm down," Dr. Green said calmly in a soothing voice as I slowly gained my composure. "Dr. Green I hate him," I cried, internally fighting with myself for showing emotion. I'd held all this emotion inside for decades and hated that I appeared so vulnerable. No one was supposed to see this side of me. This side of me was not supposed to exist. "Remember we talked about expressing ourselves through words, you have got to let go of all of this anger." I slowly got up off of the floor and sat in one of Dr. Green's office chairs. Dr. Green went back to his desk and sat down. "I'm sorry," Moneca's husband stated, still apprehensive. I didn't even bother to look at him. I was upset with Dr. Green as well. How dare this motherfucker! Over the past years, Moneca had been meeting with him for many therapy sessions and had placed a lot of trust in him. She had confided in him about all of her struggles and how this man had betrayed her. I would have never agreed to this meeting. Dr. Green was wrong for this. I protected Moneca all of this time. I kept things in order. She trusted Dr. Green, but I didn't. I had allowed her to form a bond with him and he was out of line! "What is your name?" Dr. Green asked me. What is wrong with this fool? He knows who I am. I heard him call my name earlier. "What is your name?" he asked again. A sly smile crept across my face as I leaned back in my chair and crossed my legs. "Dr. Green, you know who I am," I said, barely controlling my sinister grin. "Tell me who you are," he said as he motioned his hand towards Moneca's husband, "Tell us who you are." I paused for a moment then sat up in my chair staring Dr. Green directly into his eyes, "Ocean, mother fucker. Ocean mother-fucking Robinson." A gasp was heard come from the corner where my previous victim was standing. Dr. Green smiled, "Nice to finally meet you." I didn't respond, but only turned and glared at the man I wanted to kill. I hated him with every fiber in my body. He looked at me with sad eyes of recognition. "Ocean," Dr. Green brought my attention back to him, "Why do you hate him? "He is evil, Dr. Green. You don't know the things he has done to me. He caused Moneca so much pain. He is sick and twisted!" He turned to him, "Is this true?" He shook his head and said, "I would never do that. I love Moneca." "Liar!" I yelled, jumping up from my chair and making my way towards him. "Ocean!" Dr. Green called my name to stop me. "Ocean,

I called this meeting today to help you. I want to help you confront your past. Moneca's husband is not your enemy, Ocean." I stared straight into Dr. Green's eyes trying to understand what he was telling me. "I have someone else from your past that you need to confront." I braced myself for the worst, knowing just forty-five minutes earlier Dr. Green just had Moneca's husband confront me. I watched as he picked up his phone, alerting his secretary that it was okay to allow the unknown person to enter. I turned towards the door, awaiting the stranger's arrival. "You've got to control yourself," Dr. Green said. I turned to question him and heard the door open from behind me. Turning around, I laid my eyes on the man I thought I would never see again, the man I thought I got rid of so many years ago, the man who caused me so much hurt and pain, and the man who tried to kill me. I was blinded by fury as I grabbed the letter opener off of Dr. Green's desk and raced towards the man as he had already shut the door and entered the room. He stood there leaning on his walking cane, but the look in his eye displayed confusion, he didn't know if he should try to rush back out the door or go toe to toe with me. By the time he made a decision, it was too late. "Calm down!" he shouted, holding his hands up in a defensive manner, but I could see the treacherous smirk on his face. "Fuck you, you evil ass bastard! I hate you!" I yelled as I quickly grabbed a hold of him, pulled my arm back with so much force, and brought it forward, connecting the letter opener with his flesh. "Ocean, no!" I heard my mother yell out but, it was too late.

MONECA

Moneca felt like she needed something to live for. She was beyond tired of the hell hole that she was supposed to call home. Every day it was the same thing. Wake up at six in the morning, breakfast at eight, therapy at nine, group at ten, lunch at twelve in the afternoon, recreation at one, etc. etc. etc. She was so tired of people telling her what to do. Moneca felt like the people around her were insane, instead of her, and she didn't belong in there. Moneca had been living at the Parkside Psychiatric Unit in Austin, Texas for twenty-three years. She was forty two years old and couldn't remember what it was like to drive a car, fix a meal, or even walk down the street. It tore her up inside that she was in a facility that she knew she didn't belong in. They made her take pills, shoving them down her throat every day to keep her out of it. Every day she laid there in her bed, high out of her mind, feeling as if she was losing herself. Even though she felt that way, her daughter always stayed on her mind. She had to get back to her baby girl. Her daughter was all she had. People close and around Moneca always wondered how she ended up in a psychiatric facility. Moneca, pronounced Monica as she liked to remind everyone, Robinson's unfortunate situation began when she was just a teenager. The story goes back to a time in her life that's full of memories that she has blocked for over twenty years. The year was 1987 and the place was Oklahoma City. Back in the day Moneca was a fly, beautiful young girl. She was the hottest thing going on her block. She grew up on the Eastside of the city, where the local gangs were always beefing and dope boys kept the streets busy. They spent most of their time hanging on 23rd street trying to see who was who and who had the latest in cars and fashion. All the neighborhood boys wanted her and she knew it. You couldn't tell Moneca anything. Although she had her pick of hustlers, ballers, and shot callers, she kind of had a thing for this square boy that lived next door to her. His name was Fred Alvarez and to Moneca, he was fine. His ethnicity consisted of African-American and Mexican. He had bronze skin, silky, black hair that was cut into a Caesar fade, and he wore glasses that gave him a nerdy look. He also always appeared to be in deep thought. Fred stuck out in their hood like a sore thumb and he was not interested in joining a gang or selling drugs. He was just a quiet young man that kept to himself. Fred and Moneca grew up living next door to each other in Section eight housing off of Prospect Avenue. They played together as children, but during adolescence, she became bored with him and soon moved on to other friends. By the time they were teenagers Fred didn't have any friends and was often labeled as weird, but Moneca always loved messing with him. Fred's bedroom was directly across from hers and if the curtains were pulled back, he could see directly into her bedroom window. Moneca would purposely undress right in front of the window, just because she knew he was watching. She would laugh and wave at him as he would hurry away from the window. At eighteen, he was about six-foot-one, with a thin build and would always wear snug fitting black jeans and black t-shirts. She just knew her fast ass was going to seduce him as soon as she got a chance, but in the meantime, Fred was just too boring for her; she needed excitement. At the age of seventeen, Moneca was about five-feet and five-inches, brown skin, cute round face, dimples, and a mole right on her left cheek. She had full hips and breast when she was around thirteen, so by the time she was seventeen, she knew how to flaunt them well. All the neighborhood women called her a fast ass, but she didn't care. She was always riding around with a baller or spending his money. Her mother didn't have the energy to give a damn. She'd had a nervous breakdown when Moneca was twelve after her husband left her for her best friend. She spent most of her days rocking herself back and forth in her rocking chair in front of the television. Moneca had pretty much been taking care of herself since she was twelve. She would get her mother's disability checks in the mail, pay their bills, and was able to have the freedom to do whatever the hell she wanted. Moneca felt like she had it going on. Eventually she caught the eye of a local drug dealer named Rex, who was fine as wine. Rex kept things exciting for her and she loved every minute of it. Rex would pick her up and they would go back to his place and hump like rabbits all night long. Sex with Rex was amazing and he was always teaching her something new. She loved being around Rex, he made her feel like the bad bitch that she already knew that she was. With her mother being incapable of caring for her, she spent most of her free time with Rex when he would allow her to. She understood that he was busy and had to make his money, so she was just thankful for the time that he did allow her to spend with him. Surprisingly, she was still in school and was barely making it through her senior year at Douglas High School. Honestly, the only reason why she did show up was to show off the jewelry and new clothes that Rex would buy for her. All the females despised her and all the dudes wanted her. She figured she was going to be Rex's main girl and live comfortably off of his money. She even figured she would pop out a couple babies for him too. Moneca had her life all planned out, but Rex had a different plan. "What up sweet thang," Rex answered the phone when Moneca called him. "Rex, baby I'm getting dressed. Are you coming to get me?" "Yeah baby, but, there's a change of plans. Instead of us kicking it at my place tonight I want you to come to this party with me." "Really, baby?" she smiled thinking that Rex was finally ready to show her off as his lady. "Yes, baby. I'll be there to get you soon." Moneca hung up the phone smiling from ear to ear. She would finally be able to walk around on Rex's arm. She just knew she had him wrapped around her fingers. Walking into the living room to check on her mother, she shook her head with sadness as she looked at her. As usual, she was rocking in her chair, watching old infomercials. Moneca placed her blanket on her lap and held her glass of water to her lips. As she walked back into her room, she noticed Fred in his room sitting at his desk. Taking her shirt off, she stood there in her bra as she continued to stare at him. He finally looked up and she waved at him. He quickly looked away, but she could tell she had his attention. She took her bra off and walked up to the window. He looked up again and she lightly rubbed on her breast smiling at him. She watched as his eyes widened and he turned beet red from embarrassment. He finally got up and rushed out of his bedroom, causing Moneca to double over in laughter as she stepped back into her clothes. Walking out of her bedroom and into the living room, the loud knocking at her front door quickly startled her. "Who is it?" she yelled, walking towards the door. "It's Rex, open up," he said. She hurried to open the door as he ran up to her and pulled her into a tight, bear hug. Rex walked all the way into the house, wrapped his arms around Moneca's waist and started to kiss her neck. She giggled as he made both of them fall on the couch. She just loved being his girl. He started kissing on her neck, but she pushed him away. "Come on baby you gone mess my hair up." "I just want to spend a little time with you before we head to this party," he said in between kisses. Moneca could feel herself getting weak as her knees wobbled before she jumped off the couch. "Rex, come on baby. I spent the last hour getting pretty for you. I want you to be proud to show me off," she said as she then walked back into her bedroom to retrieve her purse.

Rex stood to his feet and followed after her. When they reached her bedroom, Rex wrapped his arms under her breasts and fell back onto her bed, with Moneca still in his arms. "Come on, sexy. Just give me what I want," he said as he tugged at her dress. Looking back at him, she couldn't help but realize how fine Rex really was. He looked like a young Idris Elba with his smooth dark skin, bald head, and full lips. He always dressed in black and white. That night he had on black jeans, a fresh white V-neck T-shirt, and white Reeboks. She couldn't fight him off any more after he slipped his fingers into her panties and caressed her love spot. She was instantly wet and squirmed as he slipped two fingers inside of her. "You know you want it," he breathed into her ear. She was on fire. He had a way of turning her all the way on. Scooting from up under her, he then got on top as she laid back on the bed and he reached between her dress and pulled her panties down. She watched him as he dropped his jeans and his dick stood straight out from his boxers. Rubbing on himself as he smiled and winked at her, she opened her legs as he moved in between them. Holding the base of his penis, he eased his way into her, making her gasp and dig her nails into his back. He teased the opening of her pussy as he bit down on his bottom lip. "You so damn tight," he groaned. She held on for the ride as Rex began to pumped faster and faster. Minutes later he was pulling out and nutting on her leg. "Damn baby, that was good," he smiled as he started to pant. "Rex, you know I love you, right?" "Yeah, baby, I know," he smiled and kissed her cheek.

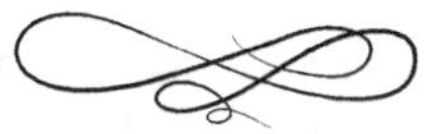

Chapter 2

MONECA

By the time Moneca and Rex walked into the house party, the party was already live. She was dressed in a tight sleeveless white dress, with red sandals, and red hoop earrings. Her long hair was pulled back into a tight side ponytail, which revealed her exotic, strong cheekbones. She had it going on. They bobbed their heads to the beat as Rex was greeted by mostly everybody at the party. Mostly everyone in the party was older than Moneca. Rex was twenty-nine and most of his friends were around his age. Her young ass was in over her head, but she didn't know it at the time. She waited alone in the hallway while Rex went into the kitchen to get them something to drink. She didn't want to go into the living room where everyone was dancing, without Rex. As she was leaning against the wall, a tall, light-skinned woman, with an up-do, bumped into her as she was walking by. She was dressed in a pair of white shorts, with a multicolored halter top on, and multicolored shoes. Turning around, she frowned her nose up at Moneca. Moneca had no idea who that woman and what her problem was. She stared at the light-skinned woman as she walked into the kitchen before waving her off. After waiting a few more minutes, Moneca decided to see what was taking Rex so long. When she entered the kitchen, the light-skinned woman was all up in her man's face, whispering in his ear. Walking up to them, she tapped him on the shoulder and asked, "Um, Rex what's going on?" Rex barely took his hands off of her as the light-skinned woman kept her arms glued around him, looked at Moneca, smiled devilishly, and asked, "Honey, aint it past your bedtime?" "Rex, who is this bitch?" Moneca spat in anger. "Bitch? Little girl don't get slapped," the light-skinned woman snapped as she looked at Rex, waiting for him to check Moneca. "Slap me then, bitch!" Moneca yelled. Pulling away from Rex, she walked up to Moneca and started pointing in Moneca's face. "I will mop this floor with your little young ass! You better watch yourself!" "Bitch, you just mad 'cause you old! Don't be mad 'cause he like this young pussy," Moneca yelled over the loud music. "Do you know what he does for a living? He ain't been doing nothing, but grooming your dumb ass." By this time, Rex decided to step in and break them up. He placed his arms around Moneca's waist and escorted her out of the kitchen. "Rex, what is she talking about?" "Baby, don't pay her no mind. She's just jealous 'cause she don't got it like you do." "Are you sleeping with her?" "Come on, sexy. Why would you even ask me something like that?" "You know why, Rex. I don't want you to be with other girls. I wanna make you happy," she stated, firmly. He smiled as he led her down the hall and into the living room. Bobby Brown's hit song, "Girlfriend", was playing on the stereo system. Rex led her to a corner in the room and placed her arms around his neck as they swayed to the song. Looking into his eyes as they danced, Moneca said, "Rex, I'm serious." "I know, baby. Listen, I'm just happy you're here with me." "Really?" she smiled up at him. She was in heaven as she laid her head on his chest in pure bliss. When the song ended, Rex took her hand and led her to the back of the home, into an empty bedroom. "So, you want to make me happy, right?" "Yeah, baby," she responded, thinking he wanted to have sex again. "Well, baby, I'm really happy when I'm getting my money." "Okay, daddy. I know you gotta get yours." "Are you down for your man?" "You know it, baby." "Daddy needs you to make this money for him." "How, baby?" she asked with confusion. A minute later, the bedroom opened and a dark skinned man with a beanie, walked into the room. Looking at Rex, she asked, "Baby, what's going on?" "Sexy, this is Slim. He just wants spend some time with you for a while." She shook her head as she started to realize what was going on. "No, Rex baby . . ." Cutting her off, he asked, "You love me, right?" "Yes, but . . ." "Daddy owes Slim a little bit of money and things would be a lot better for me if you would just show him a good time." Moneca was speechless. He kissed her cheek and whispered in her ear, "Do this for daddy, baby girl. Show daddy how much you love him." She wanted to cry as she watched Rex leave the room. He turned and winked at her, and she knew instantly that she would do anything for him. She had already convinced herself that he would love her more if she'd do what he asked her to do. Slim made his way over to her with a smirk on his face. "You're sexy as hell. Are you as good as Rex claimed?" She just smiled at him as he began to caress her legs working his way to her breasts. "You need to be on my team," he whispered in her ear as he reached into his pants, and pulled out his dick, which was as hard as a rock. Moneca's inner self took over during her interaction with Slim. It was as if she fell into a deep sleep as she blacked out the entire experience of Slim sexing her. Her body was limp and numb as she was laid there, motionless and in a daze. Slim slapped her on the ass and made his way out the room. She was ass naked lying on the bed staring at the ceiling, wondering where Rex was and forgetting that there was a party taking place outside of the bedroom. The creaking noise of the door startled her and she turned her head to see three men walk in. "Yo, is she sleep?" the first man asked. "Naw, nigga. Slim said she was up and ready," the second man said. "Nigga I'm first," the first man said. "Yo, this nigga Rex is a motherfucking pimp." She felt the bed sink under her from someone's weight as a couple of beastly hands soon felt all over her body, and between her legs. "Oh, yeah, nigga, she ready." She focused in on the three men surrounding her, staring at her like she was the last hot link at a BBQ cookout. One already had his pants down stroking his dick as she then jumped to her feet and began to scream. "You niggas get the fuck away from me!" Moneca tried to cover her body with her hands. "Yo shut up bitch, you already know what time it is," one of the men said before he grabbed her by her hair and tossed her back down on the bed. "Yo, nigga, hold her arms, this bitch like it rough." She cried as she felt her arms being pinned down on the bed. She couldn't muster up enough strength to try to fight back. Closing her eyes, she started to black out and imagine it was Rex touching on her. "I'm doing this for Rex. I'm doing this for Rex. I'm doing this for Rex!" she repeated to herself in her head as all three men mercilessly entered almost every hole in her body. She kept her eyes closed and forced herself to sleep through the whole painful experience. When she awoke, she could see sunlight coming through the blinds. She sat up and looked around the room. She was still naked and her clothes were in a corner on the floor. Did Rex leave me? How long have I been sleep?" she thought to herself. She stood up to get her clothes and her body was so sore she could barely walk. Her pussy was throbbing with pain and her anus was aching. She looked back on the bed and seen blood splatters on the sheets. What the fuck happened? She quickly dressed and left the house as fast as she could. Luckily for her, the house party they went to was on 36th and Prospect, only a few blocks from her home. She rushed home with a million thoughts racing through her mind. It was late April and the crazy Oklahoma weather had the wind whipping hard as she walked down the sidewalk with her head down trying to recall what happened. She didn't remember everything that happened, but she was certain that a train had been run on her. "But how many people?" She rushed into her house so that she could call Rex. He did not answer his phone and she hung up and called back three more times. "Rex, call me as soon as you get this message," she said, leaving him a voicemail. She checked on her mother and went to take a shower. She was trying to remember the details of last night, but couldn't. It was like she was sleeping through the incidents. "But how? I wasn't sleepy and I wasn't drinking." The next week went by very slowly. She was not able to get in contact with Rex and spent most of her time sleeping. After the incident, she'd become very ill and was running a high fever with chills and vomiting. She had no one to take care of her and she started to feel sorry for herself. She couldn't understand how Rex could do that to her. She loved him and would do anything for him. Hell, she did the unthinkable for him and he wouldn't even answer his phone. She knew that she had to see him. After a few more days, she started to feel better and was able to make her way to Rex's apartment off of 30th and Lincoln. When she arrived to his apartment, she could hear music playing inside and a female laughing. Gripped with anger, she banged on the door, causing someone to snatch it open. "Who the fuck is beating on the door?" the girl asked before she stared into Moneca's eyes. Smirking, the girl then said, "Rex, baby, you got some company." "Mona, baby, who is it?" Moneca walked into the apartment, stopping when her eyes found Rex sitting on the couch. She noticed a small baby boy sleeping in his car seat that was placed on the floor in the corner of the room. "What's up, baby?" he smiled, "You ready for more work?" "Rex, what the fuck is this bitch doing here?" Moneca yelled, pointing at

Mona. "Hold up, Moneca. You just don't walk up into my place asking me questions." "Fuck you, Rex! You just left me at that party! After I did that for you? I loved you!" She could hear Mona laughing behind her, "Baby girl, don't you get it? Rex is a pimp, he was grooming you. He was using you to make him money," Mona said as she continued to laugh. Looking at Rex with hurt and confusion in her eyes, she then asked, "What?" He shrugged and said, "Hey baby, it's a part of the game." "But Rex, I thought we had something." "We do shorty, but Mona is my main bitch, and that little boy over there," he said, pointing at the sleeping child, "is my seed. You are here to make me money. I knew you would find your way to Daddy." Moneca was at a loss for words as she continued to look at Rex with hurt in her eyes. Reaching into his pocket and pulling out a small vial of cocaine and a blade, he opened the vial, made a line of cocaine on the table, split it with the blade, and said, "Come, have a little of daddy's candy." Moneca was confused, she had never known Rex to use cocaine. She knew he smoked a little weed here and there, but never coke. He also never mentioned having a child, and he damn sure hadn't mentioned this big ass bitch, Mona. Where the hell had she been all this time that she had been laid up in his bed? Where was she when he was making love to her? She stood there, baffled as he smiled at her and kept patting the seat next to him. All of a sudden it was like a siren went off in her head and she went the fuck off. She ran over to Rex and knocked the blade and cocaine off of the table. "Fuck you nigga! You lied to me! I'm not a hoe!" Mona laughed and said, "Not from what I hear. Bitch, I heard you were working it on them niggas. You made daddy a lot of money that night. Freaky bitch took it in the ass and everything" "I was raped!" Moneca screamed. Without warning, Rex stood to his feet, and with blinded fury, hauled off and slapped Moneca before grabbing her by her neck and venomously said, "Bitch if you ever waste my shit again, I will fucking kill you!" She tried to wiggle out of his tight grip. "Since you made me money the other night, I won't hold it against you this time," he said as he let go of the tight grip he had on her neck and pushed her down to the ground. Moneca wanted to cry, but she couldn't let herself do it. She couldn't believe this was happening. All she could see was red, as she jumped up and attacked Rex. She ran at him with full force, swinging her arms wildly. She made contact with his body a few times, but not enough to hurt him. Before she could blink, Rex drew his arm back before he punched her square in her jaw. She stumbled back, but didn't fall. She grabbed her face, glaring at him with pure anger. She ran at him again and he hit her again. This time she fell back onto the floor. Rex started to beat her as Moneca then folded into a fetal position as he stomped on her. She could hear Mona laughing with every contact he made. She felt her ribs crack as his foot came down on her again and again. All she could focus on was him yelling something about disrespecting him. As she began to lose consciousness, she started wondering what the hell happened to the Rex she thought she loved.

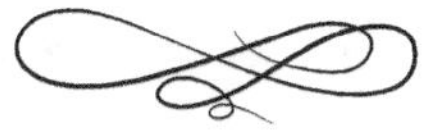

Chapter 3

MONECA

When she regained consciousness, she was laid at the top of the stairwell inside of Rex's apartment building. He had discarded her inside of the stairwell like trash. Tears came to her eyes as she stood up because every inch of her body was in pain. She still had not fully recovered from the sexual assault, and now she was sure she had several broken bones. She stumbled down the stairs in a daze. Fear stopped her from looking back to see if he was watching her. She only wanted to get as far away from there as possible. She made it down to the first floor and out of the apartment building. With every step, she cringed and cried as she walked down Lincoln Drive and then 36th street in the early hours of the morning. She held her chest as it hurt to breathe. With each step, came more pain, but she felt relief when she could see her house a block away. The pain was unbearable. Her knees became weak, and the world around her started to spin as she fell to the ground in front of her house. Tears streamed down her face and then everything went black. The sunlight was warm on her face and made her smile as she awoke. She could feel someone gently shaking her awake and she smiled again, thinking that Rex really did love her and this was all just a dream. She opened her eyes and was staring into the deepest brown and most caring eyes. Fred had a look of worry all over his face, "Moneca, Are you okay?" She tried to sit up, but cringed in pain, "Ouch." "Don't try to move, okay? What happened to you?" She looked around. She was lying on the ground outside her front door. "How did I get here?" "I don't know. I just saw your body lying on the ground. I rushed right over," Fred said. Moneca faintly remembered making it in front of her house before she passed out from the pain. "Fred can you help me in the house?" she asked. Fred picked her up in his arms in one swoop. She had no idea he was so strong. He carried her into the house and laid her on the couch. She winced in pain again. He looked at her with concern and said, "I think you need to go to the hospital. What happened to you?" She ignored him as she looked around for her mother. She grimaced as she tried to stand up. He held his hand on her shoulder to try and stop her, "You really don't need to move." "Can you check on my mother for me, please?" she pointed to her bedroom. When he came back, he asked her if she wanted to go to the hospital, again. Again, she shook her head. "Rex did this to you, didn't he?" Moneca didn't respond. "Why are you protecting him?" "Look Fred, you wouldn't understand." "Try me." "I'm in love with him," Moneca said, seriously. "You're not in love with him." "Excuse me?" "Love doesn't hurt, Moneca. Someone that loves you, wouldn't of damn near kill you." "How would you know, Fred? I mean, do you ever leave your house?" Fred, who was taken aback, remained silent. She regretted hurting his feelings, "Look Fred, I'm sorry, okay?" she said as she tried to stand to her feet, again. But due to the unbearable pain her body was bearing, it was impossible. Fred stood to his feet and said, "Look Moneca, I'm taking you to the hospital. I think you have a broken rib." Fred and Moneca drove to OU Medical Center in silence. She kept looking over at him, wondering why he was being so nice to her. Growing up, she and Fred played together all the time. The kids at school picked on him and she was probably his only friend. But after her mother had her break down and she started thinking her shit didn't stink, she dropped him like a hot potato. Fred really became an introvert after that, and she started indirectly fucking with him from her bedroom window. "Can I ask you a question?" Fred said, breaking the silence. She just looked at him. "What happened to your mother? I mean after your father left, she doesn't even leave the house anymore." "She's sick," Moneca said, nonchalantly. "What's wrong with her? I mean, when I went to check on her she was staring off into space and mumbling to herself. I don't even think she knew I was there." "My daddy left us for Lisa, my mama's best friend. My mama couldn't take it and had a breakdown. She tried to kill herself by digesting a whole bottle of pills. I was twelve when I found her passed out in our bathroom floor. When she was released from the hospital, she had been diagnosed with severe depression." "Wow, sorry Moneca. I didn't know." "It's okay. I just had to grow up pretty fast after that. The doctor's said she would be okay if she continued to attend psychotherapy and take her meds. She was never the same though. She refused to leave the house. We were able to make it without Child Protective services taking me away, but I had to take care of her. She has been getting worse over the years. I don't think it's just depression, but what can I do?" They pulled into the hospital entrance in silence. Fred went inside and a nurse came out with a wheelchair to retrieve her. "Thanks for bringing me, Fred. I really appreciate it." "I'm not leaving you. I'm going to park and I'm coming inside." She smiled as the nurse pushed her inside. Moneca hadn't been shown this kind of kindness in a long time.

She ended up being admitted to the hospital for three days. She had two broken ribs, a fractured jaw, and minor scratches, and bruises. She told the doctor that she was mugged outside of a shopping center and they seemed to believe her. Moneca also learned that she was pregnant. She was surprised to hear the news, but sad at the same time. Since she was six weeks pregnant, she knew the seed she was carrying was Rex's, but she also knew that there was no way she could go back to him. The doctor's told her that she would be considered a high risk pregnancy due to the assault and she would have to take it extremely easy. Fred stayed with her the whole time. She was really glad he was there for her. The only time he left her side was when he went to check on her mother and to attend his classes. Fred's parents had taken him out of school years ago. He'd actually earned his GED and was taking college courses at Oklahoma City Community College. Fred was everything that she should have been looking for in a man. He was kind, caring, and concerned about her well-being. Once the doctors released her, Fred took her home and helped her through my recovery. It took her weeks for Moneca to heal. By this time, Moneca and Fred had developed a natural infatuation with each other. She never wanted him to leave her side. She told him about the pregnancy and he still wanted to be with her. He wanted to raise the baby together and she was elated. She had turned all of her attention to the baby inside of her and wanted the baby more than anything. She spent most of her time imagining what it was going to be like to be a mother. Fred spent most of his time at her house, but they hadn't made love, yet. He was very timid, and she didn't think she was ready. She did love him and knew she would make love to him when she was ready.

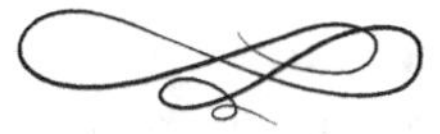

Chapter 4

MONECA

The next few weeks flew by, according to her OB/GYN doctor, she was 12 weeks pregnant and out of the first trimester. She started really focusing on the child growing inside of her and knew that she would give this child the world if she could. She didn't think about what Rex had done to her anymore, she was putting all of her love into her unborn child. She felt like God blessed her with a rainbow after a horrible storm. She was so thankful to have Fred and knew that he was nothing like Rex. She felt so much better once she was healed and able to move around easily. Fred was always on her about being careful and taking it easy. One evening, she decided to cook for Fred and if everything went as planned, she wanted to make love to him for the first time. She spent all day in the kitchen, making meat loaf, cabbage, yams, greens, and cornbread. She was so proud of herself, but really wanted to show Fred how much he meant to her. When Fred arrived, she could tell by his facial expressions that he was pleased and shocked at the same time. They both knew that in her past she had a tendency to be a self-centered bitch and so she usually wasn't surprised when people were amazed that she could do something nice for a change. After she fed her mother, Moneca and Fred sat down for dinner together. Suddenly, she was nervous about making love to him. Sex had never been about emotions to her. Although she thought she was in love with Rex, she had started fucking him long before he meant anything to her. She knew in her heart it was going to be different with Fred, and she was intimidated. Fred reached across the table and grabbed her hand, snapping her out of her thoughts. "Moneca, I've got something to tell you." "What is it?" she asked, staring him directly into his eyes. He paused as he gazed at her and replied, "I enlisted into the Air Force." She dropped his hand as his words hit her hard. "You're leaving?" she mumbled barely above a whisper. He grabbed her hand again and said, "I started talking to recruiters long before you and I became involved. If I would have known that we were going to fall for each other, I wouldn't have agreed, but it's too late." Tears rolled down her face, as she thought about their short lived romance. She didn't want him to go. She wanted him to stay and love her.

She wanted them to raise her child. She wanted him to be there. "Moneca, I have always loved you. Since we were kids. I couldn't get you out of my mind. You're everything to me. I didn't know how to tell you because I was so unsure of myself and from seeing you running around the neighborhood with all these niggas, I knew you wouldn't be interested in me. But I'm a man now, Moneca. And I'm man enough to tell you that I love you." "But you're leaving me Fred," she said as tears continued to roll down her cheeks. "We don't have to be apart, Moneca, Marry me?" "What?!" she looked at him with shock. "You want to marry me?" She watched as he pulled a ring box out of his pocket and held it in his hand. Opening the box, she smiled as she looked at the ring. It was a simple gold band. "Will you do me the honor?" he asked. The tears flowed as she accepted his proposal. "Yes!" He hugged her and kissed her all over her face. She was in heaven. She felt like she was in a dream that she didn't ever want to wake up from. She couldn't believe how much her life had changed since the incident with Rex. Fred and her unborn child were everything to her. She wrapped her arms around him, hugging him tightly. She didn't want to ever lose him. "When do you leave?" she asked as she looked up at him. "I leave in 2 weeks." "Oh my God, Fred." "Baby, we can go to the courthouse tomorrow." She smiled at him and asked, "Are you serious?" "I've never been more serious in my life," he said as he look her directly into her eyes. The next day Fred and Moneca went down to City Hall and completed their applications and paid the fees. They were so happy together. Life couldn't have gotten any more perfect for them. She couldn't believe how much her life had turned around in such a short time. She felt like she was dreaming. The plan was for her to remain home while he went to basic training and once he was assigned to his station, they would move in together. After they were married, there was no reason left for them to not make love. It definitely went down that night. Fred and Moneca took their time exploring each other's body. Their love making was so sensual it gave her goose bumps from beginning to end. He admitted to her that he was a virgin, but she didn't care, their love making was everything and more. She guided him when he hesitated, and once he was in his groove, it was mind blowing. "I love you so much," he whispered to her as he was on top of her gyrating in and out. "I love you too, baby," she gasped as she gripped his back. He placed his mouth on hers as he came and she sucked on his bottom lip as waves of pleasure took over her body as well. "We're going to be the perfect family," she kissed his chin as he rolled off of her. He wrapped his arms around her and they fell into a peaceful sleep. Hours later, sharp pains in her stomach jerked her from her sleep. She sat up in bed gripping her stomach. They felt like cramps and she thought maybe she had just eaten too much. She tried to lie back down, but the pain wouldn't subside. Fred awoke as he felt her sitting up in bed, "What's wrong, baby?" "I'm cramping bad," she cried. He sat up and looked at her. It felt like her stomach was being twisted from the inside out. She tried to sit there and let them bypass as Fred held her hand. "What is going on?" she cried. "I don't know baby, do you want to go the ER?" he asked. She shook her head as she slowly felt the pain decreasing. "I think I'm okay, I think I just need to use the restroom." She got up and made her way to the bathroom. As she sat down on the toilet and began to urinate, she suddenly felt something thick pass between her legs. She looked into the toilet and noticed a glob of blood in the toilet. She screamed and Fred came running into the bathroom. He ran to an awful sight as she stood over the toilet screaming with blood running down, in between her legs. "What happened, baby?" She didn't respond. She couldn't respond because she couldn't form the words. Her worst fear was happening and she couldn't get herself together. She dropped to the floor in a ball and cried to herself. Fred looked into the toilet and rushed out of the bathroom. He came back with the phone to his ear. She could hear him talking to a nurse on the phone. When he hung up, he told her that the hospital stated that she'd just miscarried, and she needed to be brought into the emergency room. Fred tried to clean her up the best that he could and drove her to the ER. She was silent and nearly numb the entire ride. Once examined at the hospital, the doctors again confirmed that she'd lost her baby. They stated that the mass she passed was evidence enough and she didn't require a DNC. Moneca felt they were all wrong; she didn't lose her baby. She believed that her baby was still inside of her, she could feel her. She felt that a mother knows, and she knew that she was still carrying her child. She knew they were mistaken; she knew that in time everyone would see when she gave birth to a beautiful healthy baby. They would release her in the morning and she was expected to get some rest. She hadn't spoken one word. Fred sat beside her bed, holding her hand, "Moneca, baby, we can get through this." She heard him, but she was too busy imagining herself and her child running and playing together. "Moneca, baby, say something." She silently smiled to herself as she stared out the window.

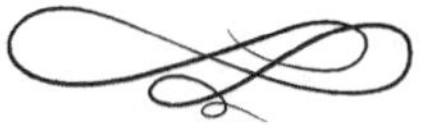

Chapter 5
ONECA

Have you ever had a feeling that some shit was about to go down? It's like a feeling in the pit of your stomach that's hard to shake. Call me paranoid if you want, but I learned a long time ago to always go with my gut feeling. You know they say when a difficult situation arises, the human being resorts to the fight or flight mentality. Well, I'm a flight type of chick. Shit! I don't play that! I don't have time for the bullshit. I've been called scary, a coward, and much worst. But, like I said, I don't give a damn! Since I was a kid, I had to stay on top of my game. I've always had a hard time trusting people and making friends. It's like people don't like me for whatever reasons and I've learned to be a loner. I prefer it that way anyway. If I got close to a person, after time passes, they just flip out! People love to accuse me of things I've never done and accuse me of saying things I have never said. I know it sounds crazy, but I'm really starting to believe I have a long lost twin out there. I've been thinking about hiring a private investigator because enough is enough! Honestly, I am a good person and I've never intentionally tried to bring harm to anyone. I was raised by my father and never knew my mother. I grew up in Aurora, CO most of my life. My father was in the Air Force, however; fortunately we were lucky to not have to move around a lot. When I was nine, he was stationed in Wichita Falls, TX, but we returned to Buckley when I was sixteen and my dad has been there ever since. He retired four years ago. After completing high school, I got accepted into the University of Colorado and moved to Denver after high school. I completed two years of school, but ended up taking a job at an Auto Insurance Company. I've been here for about five years now and I am content. I mean, I would say I'm a good catch. I'm a twenty-five-years-old beautiful woman with bronze skin, slanted eyes, and full lips. Not to mention I'm single and I have no kids. I live in a decent one bedroom apartment in Boulder, on the outskirts of Denver. Many people think that I am mixed with Asian ethnicity due to my slanted eyes, but according to my father, I am mixed with Mexican and African-American. Even though I'm a beautiful looking woman, I've always been shy, hell, let's be real, I'm uncomfortable around men. I am a twenty-five-year-old virgin. Yes, I said it; I've never had sex. Don't get me wrong, there have been men that I was head over heels for and was ready to give it up, but I never have been able to go all the way with anyone. My daddy said it was best that way, that no matter how old I got, I was his princess. But anyway, back to people accusing me of things. Frankly, some of the things people have accused me of are just baffling. I try not to worry about it and my daddy says that they are just jealous. He tells me I'm imagining the strange feelings that I sometimes get, but I know I'm not crazy. I've been having these feelings since I was eight-years-old and definitely know when to be worried. Yesterday, while I was working, I kept getting this feeling that someone was watching me. A couple of times I glanced out of our store front window and saw this guy staring at me from across the street. He looked like a thug and that's what had me worried. He was dressed in baggy jeans and a white T-shirt. He had a fitted cap on his head, but I could tell that he was looking at me. Every time I would look up, he would try to play it off and act as if he was just passing by. But, I'm not stupid. A person doesn't pass by the same street more than four times in an hour. Although I work across the street from a bank, I know his ass wasn't going in there. My daddy told me to never trust a thug, and I definitely didn't trust this one. I was ready to alert the police if I had seen him again. But, I haven't seen him since yesterday. I still couldn't shake this feeling, though. I'm sitting at my desk, wondering what I will eat for lunch today. Working as an insurance agent can have its slow days, and today was definitely one of them. The ringing phone finally gave me something to do with myself. "Thank you for calling Expedite Insurance, My name is Oneca, How can I help you today?" "Hey baby girl," I heard my father's deep voice on the other end of the phone. "Hey, daddy," I said with a smile. "Are you getting ready to go to lunch?" "Yeah, in a minute. Is everything okay?" "Yes, your daddy just wanted to check on you. When are you coming to see your old man?" "Daddy, I just came down there last weekend," I huffed. "Oh you just don't love your daddy, anymore?" "Oh come on, Daddy. I'll try my best to get down there this weekend." "Thanks, princess." "Bye Daddy, I love you," I said before ending the call. My daddy can be so possessive of my time. I love him to death, but his world circles around me. It makes it hard for me to have a life. He never remarried after my mother left us and I became the center of his existence. He's only forty-three and should be out enjoying himself and meeting new people. I don't think he's too old to get married again. It has always been hard for me to tell him no because he's all I have and I'm all he's has too.

Growing up, I was very sheltered, and my daddy was extremely over protective. Any time a kid would pick on me or accuse me of something, my daddy would say that they were just jealous of me. I really didn't begin to have social problems until I was around eight-years-old. I could tell that my teachers didn't like me, none of the kids wanted to play with me, and I would cry myself to sleep every night. My daddy was always there to comfort me. By the time I reached the age of twelve, people were just flat out mean to me. No one would speak to me unless they had to. It was hard. I definitely had a tough time growing up. I didn't have a mother, and never understood why I had so many problems. By the age of sixteen, and after we moved back to Colorado, my daddy decided to home school me. Part of the reason I decided to go to College so far away was to put some space between us and start living my own life. But, since I moved, he still manages to guilt me in to visiting him. The bell ringing above our office door snapped me out of my thoughts. I looked up and noticed a man named Mikey entering my office. Mikey is my one and only friend. He works across the street as a bank teller and over the years, we have become friends. Mikey is socially awkward, just like me. Most refer to him as a square. He always dresses in khaki pants, plaid shirts, with eyeglasses that were way too big for his face, and he is perfectly content with the penny loafers that he wears on a daily basis. If you take away his glasses and goofy low top afro, he reminds you of the actor, Mekhi Phifer. "Hi, Mikey," I greeted him as he entered the office. "Hey, 'Neca. Are you ready to get something to eat?" "Sure, let me just lock up." Mikey waited outside while I put a sign on the door and locked the office. Since we were a small company, I held down the office by myself most of the time. Our regional manager usually stopped by the office once or twice a month. This worked out well for me, since I'm not much of a people person, anyway. Mikey and I decided to have lunch at the Deli shop next door to his bank. Since it was a nice spring day, we ate our sandwiches at their tables outside. I ate my sandwich as Mikey told me how he wanted to go see this new science fiction movie coming out this Friday. Just as he was getting ready to ask me to go with him, I saw the same thug watching me from a couple of tables over. I immediately got nervous as I saw the guy make his way to our table. "Yo, what's up, O?" the thug said as he looked down at me. "Excuse me?" I asked, frowning at him. "O, baby, where you been?" "Do I know you? And why are you calling me O? My name is Oneca," I said with an attitude. "Yo baby girl, no need to front, I thought I noticed you across the street, yesterday. I'm saying, I'm just trying to link up with you again. You got some fire," the thug said as he licked his lips seductively. I almost choked on the piece of sandwich as I looked down at the ground. "I'm sorry, but I don't know you," I said completely confused and embarrassed. "Oh, so you don't know a nigga now?" he asked, frowning down at me. "Look, baby girl, I see you on your little date right now," he said, pointing at Mikey, "So why don't you just hit me up later, I still got the same number." he winked and licked his lips as he walked off. "A friend of yours?" Mikey asked, staring at me. "Mikey, I have no idea who he was," I said with a serious tone in my voice. "Well, he sure did know you," he said, matter-of-factly. "Mikey, this is some crazy shit! I really never saw this man a day in my life!" I yelled. "Well, are you going to be okay?" he asked, raising his eyebrows in concern. "No, I'm not okay. It's tripping me out that he called me O. No one has called me O since I left college five years ago." "Wow, I don't know what to say." Looking at Mikey as I shifted in my seat, I took a deep breath and said, "Mikey, I never told you or anyone else this before, but, I think I have a twin somewhere." "What?" he asked with a laugh. "I'm telling you, crazy things go on in my life, and I swear, it has to be someone out impersonating me. I had to drop out of school five years ago because of it." When he noticed I was serious, he slanted his head and asked, "What are you talking about?" "The Dean of the

Business Administration swore up and down that we had a relationship for over a year. He told his wife he was leaving her for me and everything. Mikey, I swear I barely knew the man." "Wait, Oneca that sounds crazy," he said as his eyes widened. "I know! But I swear it's true. It was a big mess. His wife was very vindictive. I kept telling them I did not have a relationship with him. I was and still is a virgin! He thought I was just trying to protect myself and then he turned on me. They reported that I was stalking him and harassing his wife. I eventually got expelled from the school. That's how I ended up here. Mikey, do you believe me?" He shrugged and nodded, "I mean I guess so. I don't think you would lie." "Mikey, I'm going to hire a private investigator to find out what the hell is going on. I can't go through this again. This happened to me in elementary and junior high. I just don't understand," I shook my head as tears started to well up in my eyes. Reaching over, Mikey wiped my tears that escaped from my eyes. I slightly smiled as he stood to his feet and threw our trash away before sitting down, again "Oneca, you're going to be fine. I will help you figure out what's going on. That's what friends are for, right?" I smiled at him. Mikey really was the only friend I had. We continued to talk until our lunch break was over.

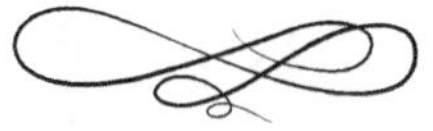

Chapter 6

ONECA

Later on that evening, I was sitting at home thinking about all the crazy twists and turns my life has taken. I never knew my mother. My father told me she ran out on us when I was two-years-old. She never came back and never contacted us again. Of course, growing up I wanted to be like other little girls and have a mother, but it didn't bother me too bad. My father did everything he could to make my life easier. Unfortunately, I never really had any friends growing up. No one ever came over for birthday parties or sleepovers. It was always just me and my father. Come to think of it, my daddy didn't have friends either. He would always say, we were just two peas in a pod. A knock at the door snapped me out of my thoughts. Standing to my feet and walking to my front door, I looked through the peephole to see who it was. My heart started racing as I saw the same thug from earlier standing on the other side. «How do you know where I live?» I yelled through the door. «Yo, O, open the door, stop playing with me,» he yelled. «Get the fuck away from my door! Or I›m going to call the police!» I shouted as I started looking around the room for my cell phone. «Why are you trying to call the police? Open the door!» he yelled, banging on the door. «What do you want?» «I got a business opportunity for you, remember you said we could make a come up?" «What are you talking about? I don't even know you!» «It›s me, girl! Remember me? My name is City. Now come on and open the door. Stop playing, girl!" I was so confused and he really did appear to know me. I don›t know if it was out of curiosity or pure stupidity, but somehow I convinced myself to open the door and see what he had to say. He came rushing in as soon as I cracked the door. «Yo, you play too much,» he said, pulling up his sagging pants and taking a seat on the couch. I was able to get a good look at him and he was sexy as fuck. His skin was almost as dark as coal. He reminded me of Tyrese as he stared at me with those slanted eyes. His body was on point. My eyes roamed his muscular forearms. I knew he was rocking a six pack under his white wife beater. As a bonus, he had several tattoos covering his arms and chest. He just screamed danger, and I was intrigued. I kept my back against the front door and my hand on the knob, just in case I needed to make a run for it. The sound of my father›s voice rung in my head as he would say to never trust a thug, which immediately caused me to tense up. «What do you want?» I asked again. He laughed, and I noticed his perfect white teeth, «Yo, shorty, are you ill or what? You don't› remember last week when I had your ass butt naked on that kitchen table?» he motioned towards my kitchen table. I crossed my arms, «Nigga you got to be crazy. I aint never had you in my house. I don›t even know you.» Walking towards me, he said, «So, you really don›t know me, huh?» I shook my head as he slowly walked towards me. «So, you don›t remember this?» he asked as he took my hand and placed it in his pants, forcing me to run my fingers up and down his penis. That shit felt so good, I instantly got wet. I stared at him as I kept my hand on his crouch, unable to move. «And you don›t remember this?» he asked as he began to lick on my neck. My legs started to wobble uncontrollably as a soft moan escaped from my lips. Next thing I knew, City had dropped to his knees, pulled my shorts down, and was nibbling on my pussy through my cotton panties. I knew this wasn›t right, but I couldn›t form the words to tell him to stop. He placed my legs, one by one, on his shoulders and I was forced to lean against my front door. He entered one finger and then two inside of me, causing my juices to come flowing out. "Oh yeah, you remember," he smiled. I gasped as he began to dart his tongue across my clit. I grabbed the back of his head, unable to remember my own damn name while he was so worried about me remembering his. He swirled his tongue around my clit and I lost all control of any common sense that I had left at that moment. He continued to move his fingers in and out of me as he rotated between sucking and licking my clit. I swear I saw Jesus as his fingers and tongue got faster and faster. "Come for me baby," he said in between licks. I closed my eyes and cried out as pleasure rippled through my body. I collapsed on top of his shoulders as all of the energy escaped from my body. A moment later, I shook my head as I opened my eyes and jumped out of his grip. "Stop, stop!" I yelled out. "I gave you what you wanted," he said as he stood to his feet and wiped his mouth. "Naw, hell no. This was a mistake," I exclaimed. "Yo, you playing hard to get. But, it's cool," he said reaching down his pants and pulling out his rock hard penis, "I know how to set you straight." My eyes were fixated on his member. There was a reason why I was a virgin and those instincts kicked in immediately. I was terrified. "You gotta go," I said, looking away. His eyes were full of disbelief as I opened the front door while he stood there holding his throbbing penis. He put it back in his pants and made steps towards me. "I'm not gone keep playing these games with you," he said in an angry tone. "Get the fuck out!" I slammed the door as soon as he stepped out of it and I could hear him cursing my name all the way down the hallway.

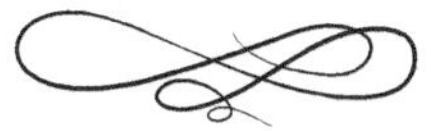

Chapter 7

MONECA

"Moneca, it's almost time for your session with Dr. Green," the blonde nurse said, startling Moneca when she poked her head into her room. Moneca turned to her and nodded. "Would you like for me to walk with you to his office?" "No, I can manage," Moneca said. She'd been sitting on her bed, writing in her diary. As always, her daughter was on her mind. Moneca knew she has grown into a beautiful young lady. She couldn't believe that Fred had her committed to that psychiatric facility and has never bothered to bring her home. She wrote him letters, constantly begging him for at least a picture of her daughter. Fred never responded to any of her letters. He used to come and visit when she was first admitted, but he hasn't come to visit her in over fifteen years. When he did visit, Moneca would ask him about their daughter and ask him to bring her, but he never complied. She had no idea why he turned on her. She would have never thought that Fred could be so cruel. He committed the ultimate betrayal; he ripped a mother away from her child. Moneca's walk to Dr. Green's office was brisk. She kept my head down and didn't make eye contact with anyone. When she first came to live there, she was so distraught that she barely talked or trusted anyone. But after realizing that her chances of going home were nearly slim to none, she formed a bond with a woman named Kina. For a while, Moneca and Kina were really good friends. Kina felt that she was wrongfully admitted too. She was accused of attempting to kill herself by driving her car into a river with her kids in the car. After getting to know Kina, Moneca had never seen her act strangely and felt as if she was as normal as her. She thought she was just like her and had been falsely placed here and held against her will. After months of Moneca and Kina hanging out, playing cards, and watching television, Kina began to change. She would sometimes talk to herself while other times, Moneca would catch her laughing at herself hysterically. Moneca would ask her who she was talking to and she would say her brother. She shook it off thinking that maybe her brother had passed away and that was her way of staying connected to him. Moneca figured she would talk about it when she was ready. Kina showed the same respect for her when it came to talking about her daughter. One day, Moneca and Kina were sitting in the community room watching television. Kina was rocking in her chair and every so often would let out an uncontrollable giggle. At that point, Moneca was starting to feel uncomfortable around her. She kept looking at Kina out the corner of her eye, wondering if maybe she really was crazy. The Lord only knew she had discovered this about a few others who were living in the facility with her. There was Omar, who she believed was certified psychopath. He would walk up and down the hallway totally naked, citing verses from the bible. The general rule was to never make eye contact with him. If you did, he would mistake that for admiration, and you would find yourself being humped on by a two hundred pounds, fifty year old lunatic, while being quoted verses from the bible. Another psychopath was a girl named Big Shirley. She weighed about four hundred pounds and would eat your arm off if you let her. Big Shirley would walk to and from the cafeteria all day long awaiting meal times. You could always hear her coming because her breathing was as loud as a freight train. Moneca swore it sounded like she was snoring when she was awake. One day, Big Shirley sat next to her in the cafeteria, and Moneca had to keep looking over at her to make sure she hadn't fallen asleep because she was snoring so damn loud. That was the same day her big ass started sucking on Moneca's shoulder when she briefly looked away. Moneca slapped her head away from her and got up and moved. Delly was another one, but she had a witty personality. She was always singing Whitney Houston songs and swore up and down she used to be married to Pat Sajek. She claimed she met him as a contestant on Wheel of Fortune and he promised her he would help launch her singing career. Word on the street was that Delly had been living in mental health institutions since she was a little girl. Moneca remember when she couldn't stop laughing when a nurse named Jackie decided to mess with Delly and insisted on confronting her on her delusional stories every chance she got. The rest of them usually just let Delly tell her stories and then throw out a few questions as if they actually believe her lies. But one day, Jackie got mad when Delly was telling them how she performed on Good Morning America. She was vividly acting out her dance routine on a song she had written and accidentally backed into Jackie who was entering the room. The medication tray that Jackie was carrying went flying and everyone's pills were all over the floor. Although Delly immediately apologized and began to pick up the pills, Jackie wasn't accepting her apology and was livid. "Got damn, Delly! You crazy bitch! What's wrong with you?" Jackie yelled. "I'm sorry,

Jackie. I'll pick them up," Delly said as she frantically got on her knees and started picking up the pills. "Move, fool. Get your nutty ass over there away from them," Jackie shooed at Delly with her foot. Delly stood to her feet, looking as if she wanted to cry as she then said, "Well Jackie you don't have to be mean." "Yeah, you ain't gotta be a bitch about it!" Kina yelled at her. "You stay out of this, Kina! Or I tell your doctor you need to start taking your injections again," Jackie spat at her, causing Kina to close her mouth quickly. "Jackie, I was just showing them my dance routine that I did on Good Morning America," Delly explained as she started dancing to an unknown beat in hear head, "You know my husband got me that spot on the show." "Oh, shut up, Delly. Everyone knows your ass wasn't married to any Pat Sajak! That man don't want you!" "You shut up, Jackie! I was married to him!" Delly exclaimed. "Delly, you're bipolar. Everyone knows it. No one believes your bullshit ass stories. You hallucinate and you obsess over random ass shit. The sooner you realize it, maybe they'll would let your crazy ass out of here. Oh, wait, no, that's not gone happen. Since you been institutionalized since you were twelve-years-old, your parents didn't even want to deal with your ass no more," Jackie said, heartlessly. Delly just stood and stared at Jackie, not uttering a word. Everyone quietly waited for Delly's response. Jackie began to feel uncomfortable as Delly continued to look at her emotionlessly. "Oh, you don't have anything to say?" Jackie asked, finally breaking the silence. As Delly stood there, quiet and without an dead-pan-stare, a moment later she started urinating on herself, in which she was also known for. But before anyone else could blink, Delly hauled off, grabbed Jackie by her throat, and pulled her wig off. Pushing Jackie away, Delly then started to make a run for it. "I'm every woman, it's all in meeeeeee," she sung as she skipped down the hall, waving Jackie's wig in the air. "Oh my God!" Moneca laughed hysterically. Everyone in the room started laughing. Kina was leaning onto Big Shirley as they both were doubled over in laughter. Jackie placed her hands over her head and ran off in embarrassment. Those were a few good experiences Moneca remembered in the horrific situation she was in. Even though she was in that situation, she had to learn how to make the best of it. There was another situation she couldn't help but think about. One day her and Kina were sitting in a room together when Kina started laughing out of the blue. Moneca eyed her and asked, "What's so funny?" "Girrrlllllll" she prolonged the word then giggled again. Moneca frowned up her nose. "Kina, girl I'm getting ready to send you over there with Delly," she said, pointing over to a nearby corner where Delly was sitting.

"The devil made me do it," she whispered. "The devil made you do what?" Moneca asked. "The devil is brother," she said. "Kina, what the hell are you talking about?" Moneca asked, cutting her eyes at her. "The devil, my brother, be making me do stuff," she said, leaning in closer to her. "Like what Kina?" Kina then aimlessly looked into the air and replied, "My kids were the devil, he wanted me to bring them to him." "Kina are you saying you killed your kids?" She looked over at Moneca and nodded her head. Anger gripped Moneca as she clenched her teeth. Standing to her feet, Moneca said, "Bitch, are you crazy?" She then reached back and tried to slap Kina but Kina quickly moved out of the way. Kina started to cry, causing one of the nurses to run over to them. "What's going on, Moneca?" "This bitch is crazy," Moneca said, walking away. By the time Moneca finally made it to Dr. Green's office, she felt a little at ease. Her sessions with him were one of the few times she could actually let her guard down in that place. She'd been meeting with Dr. Green for over a year now. The previous psychiatrist over the years didn't really help her, but when the facility hired Dr. Green, he really started to make a difference in her life. Anytime Moneca mentioned her daughter's name to any of the previous doctors, they would always end up sedating her. Dr. Green was different. He would allow her to talk about her daughter for as long as she wanted. "Come on in," he called after she knocked on his door. She took a seat in one of his chairs, placed in front of his desk. Dr. Green was an older black man with salt and pepper hair. He had a medium built and always wore sweater vests and khaki pants. He kept a picture of his wife and his thirty-year-old son on his desk. Moneca always felt herself looking at their picture a little too much. "Dr. Green, I've been thinking about something," Moneca finally said. "What's that?" he asked. "I think I'm ready for you to read my diary." "What made you change your mind?" he asked. "I need to get out of here! I just want you to understand I'm really not crazy!" "Moneca, do you understand why you been here for so long?" he asked, sincerely. "Their trying to say weird things." "And what is that?" "That my daughter isn't real." "But, she isn't, Moneca," Dr. Green said, leaning forward in his desk. "Dr. Green, she is real and I'm not crazy," Moneca said, clenching her teeth. "Moneca we've been through this several of times. You had a nervous breakdown when you miscarried twenty five years ago. Your husband Fred tried to work things out with you, but you just got worse as the years went on. After so long, he didn't know what to do, so he brought you here. " "Dr. Green, Fred is lying! He kept my daughter! She is real!" Moneca cried. Dr. Green took his glasses off and rubbed his eyes in frustration. Taking a deep breath, he then said, "Moneca, the sooner that you come to terms with reality, the sooner you will go home." Moneca just stared at him. She was starting to think that she just needed to give these people what they wanted and pretend as if my daughter wasn't real. "Moneca, I have spoken to Fred on the phone recently." "What did he say? Where is my daughter?" "Do you remember what happened to you right before you and Fred decided to become a couple?" Eyeing him with confusion, she shook her head. "Do you remember the men who assaulted you?" She shook my head again before she dropped her head into her palms and started to think. A few moments passed until there was a faint image of three men standing around me and looking down on her. But she couldn't clearly remember what Dr. Green was referring about. A moment later, her body started shaking uncontrollably and her mind took her to another place. She took a deep breath before everything around her went black. About five minutes later, she opened her eyes again, while she tried to catch her breath. When she frantically looked around, she noticed she was being dragged from Dr. Green's office by two male attendants. "What's going on? What happened?" she cried. Dr. Green was standing near her with his shirt ripped and his glasses were broken and on the ground. He looked down at her with concern.

"You don't know what just happened?" he asked. Moneca shook her head and looked up at him with confusion. "Moneca who were you just now?" Dr. Green asked. "What do you mean?" she asked with her eyebrows raised. Before he can answer her, a nurse came into his office and injected a needle into her. She looked at Dr. Green one last time before drifting off to sleep.

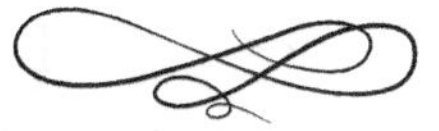

Chapter 8

ONECA

knock at my door caused me to awake from my sleep. Looking at my alarm clock, I sat up in bed wondering who could be knocking on my door so early in the morning on a Saturday. As soon as I lifted the covers off of me, I panicked when I noticed I was naked. I never slept naked. My sheets were filled with the scent of a man's cologne. The scent was familiar but, I could not place it. I sat frozen in a daze for a moment wondering where the hell my clothes were. The knocking continued as I stepped out of bed and held my head. The room was spinning and I had a pounding headache. I was able to throw on a pair of shorts and a T-shirt and make my way into my living room where I found the remnants of what looked like a party for two. There were two glasses sitting on my coffee table next to an empty bottle of Hennessy. There was also a half smoked blunt laying on the table, along with an ashtray full of cigarettes. "What the hell happened last night?" I thought to myself making my way towards the front door. I finally opened it. Standing on the other side was smiling Mikey. "I've got good news," he said, making his way into my apartment. He was dressed in a pair of khaki shorts and a green and yellow plaid Ralph Lauren shirt. "Whoa, looks like you had a good time last night," he said, looking at my coffee table. He watched me as I made my way into the kitchen looking for some aspirin. Apparently, I was having a hangover. "Mikey, what brings you by so early in the morning?" "I found a private investigator for you," Mikey said. "Oh, wow. Really?" I asked with shock. "Yeah, you know, you sounded really worried when you were telling me about the things that have been happening to you, and I just wanted to help out," he said as he handed me the business card. "Mikey you are right on time," I said as I took a seat on my couch with a bottle of water. Popping the aspirin into my mouth and taking a few sips of water, I held my head as I took a deep breath. "What's wrong?" he asked as he took a seat next to me. "Mikey, I don't know what's going on with me! I swear, I don't remember drinking and smoking last night. But, look at my house," I said, pointing around. "Oneca you need someone to help you figure this entire thing out." "I know," I replied. "This private investigator can meet with you today." "Okay, because I really need some answers, Mikey." He stood to his feet and asked, "Can I use your restroom?" "Yeah, you know where it is," I said, running my fingers through my hair and reading over the business card that read Nathan P. Hart, P.I. Hopefully, he would be the answer to my problems. A few moments later, Mikey returned to the living room. "I thought you had to use the restroom? That was fast," I said, looking up at him. He had an uncomfortable look on his face and said, "I'll just use it at home." He then made his way to the front door. "Call me after you meet with the PI." "You're not going with me?" I asked. "No, I think you can handle it. Look Oneca, I'll just see you later, okay?" he said as made his way out the door. What the hell was wrong with him? I decided to clean up the living room first, then shower and dress so that I could go meet with the P.I. When I walked into the bathroom, I immediately noticed what must have made Mikey extremely uncomfortable. There was a used condom lying on the bathroom sink that was full of semen. "What the fuck?!" I immediately knocked it into the trash can and disinfected the bathroom sink. I undressed and got into the shower as I picked through my brain, trying to figure out what happened last night. Did someone have sex in my home last night? It couldn't have been me. I know I'm still a virgin; I have to be. I ran my hand over my vagina and shivered at how sensitive my clitoris was to the touch. I closed my eyes as the warm water ran down my body, trying to recall what may have taken place last night. Did I have sex with someone? As the hot water cascaded down my body, I couldn't stop touching myself. I couldn't get over how good my touch felt. I kept my eyes closed as I pressed my clitoris with two fingers. I was ashamed at what I was doing, but I couldn't stop. I raised one leg onto the ledge of the bath tub and quickened the pace of rotating my fingers back and forth around my clit. I lifted my left hand to my nipple which was throbbing, but firm. I slowly caressed my left nipple. I then inserted my right index finger into my opening and was taken aback at how wet I was. Using my right middle finger, I begin to apply pressure to my clit, again. I remembered how good it felt to have City's mouth down there and threw my head back in bliss. I couldn't hold in the moans as I quickened my pace and rapidly rubbed on my clit, not wanting to stop for anything. My leg began to shake uncontrollably and I had to hold on to the towel rack so that I wouldn't fall. I cried out in relief as all the tension that had been building from my toes to my chest slowly erupted from my body. I again inserted my finger into my vagina amazed at how it pulsated around my fingers. When I was done, I stepped out of the shower feeling a lot better. Wrapping my towel around myself, I then walked into my bedroom. A half an hour later, I was dressed in black skinny jeans and a black T-shirt. My hair was pulled into a messy bun on top of my head and my large Chanel glasses were covering most of my face. I clutched my BCBG bag as I made my way out of my front door.

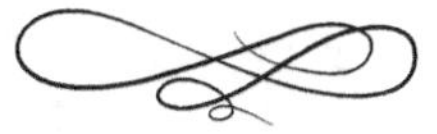

Chapter 9

ONECA

Moments later, I arrived at the P.I.'S office and walked in. When I walked in, there was an older white man sitting behind a desk in the corner of the room. He had his feet kicked up on top of the desk and he was watching a baseball game on television on the adjacent wall. He was a bit over weight and he looked like he hadn't shaved in weeks. He was dressed in a gray T-shirt and was wearing a black and purple Rockies baseball cap. "Can I help you?" he asked, not even bothering to take his feet of the desk. "Yes, my name is Oneca Alvarez, and I was given your information by a friend of mine," I said as I took my sunglasses off and placed them into my purse. "You must be Mikey's friend," he said. I looked down at him and nodded. "Well, take a seat," he said as he waved his hand towards the only chair in the room right in front of his desk. I took a good look around his office before I sat down. It was damn near empty with only his desk, the one chair, and a television Stand. "My name is Nate and I've been in the business for twenty years." "Well, Nate, I really hope you can help me," I said. "Why don't you start from the beginning and don't leave anything out." he said while pressing record on a handheld recorder sitting on his desk. He also pulled out a pen and pad. I proceeded to give him a rundown of my life beginning at around age of eight. By the time I finished telling him, he had some questions for me. "Tell me more about your father." "What do you want to know?" "How would you describe your relationship with him?" "Well, we're very close to an extent. My dad is a man of very few words, but he's there for me when I need him. He is very dependent on me, too." "What do you mean?" "I mean, his life revolves around me. Like I said before, my mom left us when I was two-years-old, and my dad has put all of his focus into me ever since. He's very protective over me, too." "Tell me about your mother?" "I don't know much about her," I shrugged. "I don't even remember her. My dad doesn't even have a picture to show me." "Why not?" I shrugged, "He says that when she left, he got rid of it all." "Why do you think he did that?" "I guess because he was so hurt by her leaving. Honestly, I don't know" "Do you ever ask him about it?" "No. Only because I can tell it makes him uneasy and sometimes he gets upset."

"Well, Ms. Alvarez," Nat said as he turned his recording device off, "I think you have given me plenty of information to start with. I'm not sure what it is that you want me to discover, but I will be putting surveillance on you and some of the people who are close to you." I nodded, "Should I let them know?" "I would suggest that you didn't. Only because you obviously have no clue what is going on in your life and we want to make sure that all parties are innocent." "Okay." "My retainer is five hundred dollars. After I conclude my investigation, you will be billed for all remaining expenses." Reaching into my purse, I then took a pen and my check book and wrote a check. When I was done, I gave it to him and watched as he stared at it before he said, "I do have one suggestion though." "Okay and what's that?" "I need to ask your dad for more information about your mother. I know you don't want to upset him, but I feel like she is a key component to this investigation" I nodded again, already trying to figure out how I could approach my father about Nate's request before I stood to my feet and shook his hand. Since being awaken early this morning by Mikey, I'd had plenty of time to get my day going. I had already met with the P.I. and it still wasn't even noon yet. I decided that I might as well hop on the highway and go visit my dad. I know that if I kept procrastinating about asking him about my mother, then I would eventually wouldn't do it. Plus, he had asked me to come visit him anyway. The drive from Boulder to Aurora was a forty five minute ride and it gave me some time to think and clear my head. The unknown incident that happened yesterday had my going half crazy. I mean, between my run-ins with City and my recent sexual feelings, I just didn't understand what was going on with me. I arrived at my father's house at one in the afternoon. I parked my car beside his silver Chevy F-150 with his retired Air Force bumper sticker on it that was shining in the sunlight. I used my key to enter and found him doing his usual lunch time routine, eating a ham and cheese sandwich and watching Sanford and Son. "Hi, daddy," I greeted him. He looked up surprised to see me as he then smiled and said, "Oneca, you came to see your old man?" My father looked younger than his forty-three years. Being of mixed heritage, his black and Mexican ethnicity gave him a bronze complexion and deep brown eyes. He kept his naturally dark curly hair cut short like the military had required of him during his time served. He was dressed in pair of old black pants with a gray cotton T-shirt on. Walking over to him, I embraced him as we then gave each other a tight hug. "I'm surprised you're not watching the news," I said as I pulled away from him. "Why is that?" "Well, I just heard on the radio about the recent shootings at the movie theater here at that Batman movie." "I know," he shook his head, "Ain't that just terrible?" "Yes it is," I said before changing the subject. "Daddy, how have you been?" "I'm alright, baby girl. I mean my blood pressure has been a little high, but nothing I can't handle." "Daddy you better take care of yourself, you're all I got," I said with a serious tone. "I know, baby. Don't you worry about me, okay? You're daddy's not going anywhere, anytime soon. Who do you think is going to protect you from those nappy headed niggas?" he said with a smile. I laughed and replied, "Daddy, I'm twenty-five-years-old, you don't need to protect me. I got this. You know I'm a big girl." "I know, but it doesn't matter. No matter how old you get, I'll always protect you," he said seriously. "Daddy, you don't have to worry about me. I know you'll always protect me, though. That's what fathers are for." "It's not you that I'm worried about," he said as he finished up his sandwich. "It's these thugs and hoodlums." "Now Daddy you taught me a long time ago not to trust them." "Yeah, but, you're a beautiful woman, Oneca. They're going to be after you, no matter what." "But I don't want them." "Don't matter," he said, standing up, "Your mama made the same mistake." I watched him as he took his plate into the kitchen. I was surprised that he mentioned my mother. He rarely ever brought her up. I felt like this was my chance to talk to him about her. I watched as he walked back into the living room, glance out of the window, and took a seat back on the couch. "Daddy, what do you mean about Mama?" "Never mind that," he said, waving me off by turning the volume up on the television. "You want to watch something else?" he asked. "No, daddy," I said getting up to turn the television off, "I want to talk about my mother." He immediately became agitated, "You know everything there is to know, she left us," he gritted. "But, Daddy, have you heard from her at all? I find it odd that she just left and we haven't heard a peep in twenty three years. "What? Are you calling me a liar?" he exclaimed, slamming his hand down on the arm of his recliner. I sighed and replied, "No, daddy. I just want to know about my mother. I'm a grown woman and don't even know what she looks like. You won't even tell me anything about her! Come on daddy!" "What's the point of knowing anything about her? She's not coming back!" he said, heartlessly. "How do you know Daddy?" "Because she's not!" he yelled. He stood up and headed towards the front door before he turned around and said, "You can be so damn selfish sometimes! I raised you by myself, Oneca. I gave you everything that you ever asked for, and all you do is move away. You act like you never want to visit and now you're accusing me of lying to you about your mother?"

"Daddy, I love you for all of those things, but, you can't make me forget about her!" I yelled as tears formed in my eyes. "Then I think its best that you leave," he said, opening the front door. After I sat there looking at him with shock and disbelief, he decided to leave himself. "It would be best that you not be here when I get back," he said before leaving out the front door. Tears rolled from my eyes as I watched through the window as he got in his truck and drove off. I couldn't believe the way my father was acting. Why did my mother leave? I needed answers. After a short period of time, I was able to pull myself together and decided to go ahead and leave and give my daddy what he asked for. I didn't know how we would recover from this. He had never spoken to me like that before, but, then again, I have never pushed so hard for information about my mother. I walked out to my car, locking the front door behind me. As I was walking to my car, I heard someone say, "Damn baby you fine." I turned around to see a little boy who couldn't be more than twelve-years-old, standing in my dad's front yard. "You look like New-New" he said. He was dressed in pair of jeans that he was purposely sagging and showing off his red and gray underwear. He had a on a red V-neck T-shirt and a red Chicago Bulls fitted cap on his head. "Excuse me?" I asked, surprised to see him standing there. "I said baby you look like New-New but better," he said again as he licked his lips. "Who is New New?" I asked. "You know, on that movie, ATL." "Oh, you mean Lauren London?" I laughed at this little boy. This was not the first time that I had been told that I resemble the actress but I was amused that this little kid was brave enough to walk up in my yard to approach me. "Yeah, you just a little darker," he stated. "But, I like you and I definitely like my women thick." "Boy, take your little ass home," I said as I started making my way to my car and laughing at the same time. "Little ass? Baby I'm all man," he said, offensively. "How old are you?" I asked. Before he could answer, Ms. Jones, my father's neighbor, came walking up the driveway. "Trey, get your bad ass out of their yard!" she yelled. "Ah, come on Grandma! I'm just laying down a little game real quick!" She laughed and said, "Boy, if I have to tell you again, I'm gone go find a switch." He trotted out of the yard, holding his sagging pants up as he moved, "Call me, baby!" he yelled before disappearing around the shrubs. I walked up to Ms. Jones and gave her a hug. "How are you, baby?" she asked. "I'm good. How have you been?" "Just fine, sugar. These grandkids keeps me on my toes," she laughed. I laughed, too. "He was a mess. But, very handsome." "Were you stopping by to visit your daddy?" she asked. "Yes, Ma'am." I then watched as she reached in her back pocket and pulled out a letter.

"Oh, okay, good. That crazy mailman of ours got our mail mixed up, again. He delivered this to my house by mistake. Will you make sure your daddy gets it?" she asked. I took the letter from her and glanced down at the sender. Moneca Robinson-Alvarez. "I know it's always good to hear from your mama isn't it honey?" I nodded as I looked down at the letter with confusion. "Your mama was so beautiful, sugar. You look just like her," Ms. Jones said with a smile. "We were all surprised when your daddy had her taken away. But, honey, she needed that help. It was either that or jail for her. She was acting very bizarre that last year before she was taken away." Ms. Jones shook her head as her memories came to her. "Back then, I didn't live next door to your dad but, I still lived in the neighborhood. You're daddy stayed for a few years, but was eventually transferred to Texas. I'm glad you guys ended up back here." I just smiled back at her as my heart sunk into my stomach. "Thanks, Ms. Jones. I'll make sure he gets it." I couldn't wait to read the letter.

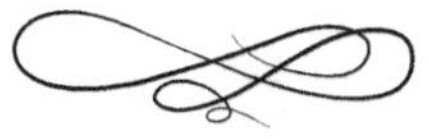

Chapter 10

MONECA

Moneca had been confined to her room for the past two weeks. Supposedly, she attacked Dr. Green during their last session. Awkwardly, Moneca didn't remember attacking Dr. Green. If being confined to her room was supposed to be punishment and torture, Moneca knew it had definitely served its purpose. With the time she'd been confined to her room, she'd been using the time to write in her diary. She also decided to write another letter to Fred, pleading for him to get her out of the horrible conditions she was living in. For the first time in two weeks, Dr. Green finally agreed to have another session with Moneca, since denying her other requests. Moneca was nervous, hoping and praying she wouldn't black out and wake up with nurses sedating her while they claimed that she attacked Dr. Green, again. She didn't know how she could control her unusual behaviors when she didn't even know how they were even happening. When she finally was ready to go see Dr. Green, she took a deep breath, walked out of her room, and made her way to his office with her head held low. She gripped her diary tightly in her hand as she said a silent prayer in her head. When she finally reached Dr. Green's office, she briefly closed her eyes as she knocked and opened his office door. Dr. Green smiled as Moneca entered his office and took a seat in front of his desk. "Good Morning," he said pleasantly. "Good morning," she replied barely above a whisper. "Moneca, I feel like we are finally going to make some progress." "Oh, yeah? Why is that?" she asked, slanting her head as she looked at him. "When you were first admitted to this facility, you were diagnosed with Delusional Disorder." She nodded, remembering when her previous psychiatrist mentioned that to her years ago. "Your previous psychiatrist, along with your husband, reported that you believed that you had a daughter, but you actually don't have one. You also kept thinking that you had her in your life for two years and that you were actually raising her. What actually was happening was you were just imaging it. When someone actually tells you that those events didn't really happen, you become irate and violent. Before you were admitted here, your husband stated that you were acting very much delusional. He also stated that you were walking the streets crying out for your daughter and in a bad daze." "That's crazy," Moneca growled. "Fred is lying! Why would he let me carry on for two years pretending that my child existed? I specifically remember holding her, feeding her, and loving her!" "Fred stated that he knew you had been through a lot and he knew you were very fragile, so he let you continue on and allowed you to pretend that you had a child for two years. He reported that he let you decorate a bedroom in pink and purchase toys. He would let you talk about her and pretend as if she was there, but she never was. He just always thought that you would snap out of it, but you never did. Fred stated that it became a problem when others began to notice, too. You were never social, so you didn't really have any friends. But, the neighborhood began to notice your strange behaviors. You would push an empty stroller down the street. You would sit at the park behaving as if your daughter was with you. So when that happened, Fred finally admitted you here." "Dr. Green, this is crazy, I just don't understand," Moneca said with tears in her eyes. "Moneca, I know this all sounds ludicrous. That's because no one has ever been open with you about this information. I've decided to try a different approach with you. I want to be open with you about everything and I want to include your input in your treatment here. I want you to help me, help you." "Dr. Green, I have a daughter! I have a daughter! I have a daughter!" she cried as she repeated over and over again. "You had a miscarriage, Moneca. You never had a daughter. Do you remember giving birth?" She slowly shook her head, desperately trying to remember the day she brought her daughter into this cold, dirty world. "That's because you never experienced it. Fred reports that you changed after your miscarriage. You were almost in a comatose-like state. You barely talked; you didn't do much of anything. You were almost a zombie, Moneca. Only existing, not living. According to my notes, your mother went through a similar situation, but she recovered from it. Fred assumed you would too. He had enlisted in the Air Force and eventually had to leave for basic training. When he came back, you had gotten worse. He was transferred to Aurora and you went with him. He said, one day you just snapped out of it, but you began to speak about your child. You would ask him to keep his voice down so that he wouldn't wake the baby. You would spend all your time in this makeshift nursery that he allowed you to make. As time went on, you'd gotten worse, Moneca. He finally decided to sit you down and try to explain to you that your daughter was not real. That is when you became uncontrollable. You would lash out at him, you attacked one of your neighbors, and you would cry for hours at a time." Moneca began to cry as she sat there, desperately trying to think of something that she could prove to Dr. Green that her daughter was real. Dr. Green looked at her with sympathy in his eyes. She then watched as his he eyed her diary. "You brought your journal today?" he asked. She nodded as she wiped her tears with the back of her hand. "Are you ready to let me read it?" She nodded as she handed it to him over his desk. I did not understand why this was happening but I just knew that I trusted Dr. Green and I wanted to get better. I watched Dr. Green place my journal in his top drawer. "There's something else that I want to discuss with you," he said. "I don't believe you have Delusional disorder." Eyeing him with confusion, Moneca asked, "What do you mean?" "Delusional disorder is characterized by the presence of non-bizarre delusions, which have persisted for at least one month. Non-bizarre delusions typically are beliefs of something occurring in a person's life which is not out of the realm of possibility. For example, their significant other is cheating or that someone is out to get them, or in your case, that they have a child. All of these situations could be true or possible, but the person suffering from this disorder knows them not to be. People who have this disorder generally don't experience a marked impairment in their daily functioning in a social, occupational or other important setting. Outward behavior is not noticeably bizarre or objectively characterized as out-of-the-ordinary. The delusions can't be better accounted for by another disorder, such as schizophrenia, which is also characterized by delusions, which are bizarre. The delusions also cannot be better accounted for by a mood disorder, if the mood disturbances have been relatively brief." Dr. Green paused to look at me. "Are you following me?" She nodded, but was still very confused. "Moneca, I don't believe that schizophrenia has not been fully ruled out." "You think I have schizophrenia?" "Yes, I do. I believe you have met Criterion A for Schizophrenia, with the delusions and hallucinations. I believe you have a mild case of it, but, in general, I think you have it. Your behavior is not obviously odd or bizarre. Schizophrenia is a mental disorder that is typically makes it hard to tell the difference between what is real and not real, think clearly, have normal emotional responses, and act normally in social situations. In your case, your only struggle is identifying what is real and what is not real. You're history of not thinking clearly, extraordinary emotional responses, and bizarre behavior in social situations have all been related to your delusions and hallucinations. Certain events may trigger schizophrenia in people who are at risk for it, because of their genes. You are most likely to develop schizophrenia if you have a family member with the disorder, too. Schizophrenia symptoms usually develop slowly over months or years. People with any type of schizophrenia may have trouble keeping friends and working. Another rare symptom is the development of multiple personalities. There is a presence of distinct or split identities or personality states that continually have power over the person's behavior. There's also an inability to recall key personal information that is often explained as forgetfulness. There are also highly distinct memory variations, which fluctuate with the person's split personality." Moneca stared at Dr. Green in disbelief. He really thinks I have a split personality? She thought to herself. Dr. Green pulled several pamphlets from his desk and handed them to me. "Moneca, I believe you are a very intelligent woman. I want to give you this information so that you can read it for yourself. I know all of this is hard to digest right now, but I believe over time you will begin to realize that there is hope for you. I want us to work together so that you can be healthy again and return home. The presence of multiple identities seems extreme to you right now but keep in mind that the host personality is usually unaware of the alter identities. I believe you experienced some trauma in your past that has influenced you to develop another identity so that you may escape from reality." "I've never experienced anything that was traumatic," she said. "Not according to your husband." "What did he say?" "Moneca, we will work our way there with time. I don't want to rush your treatment. There is hope for you. I would like to complete more assessments with you to determine an accurate diagnosis. With medications and psychotherapy, you can function as a normal adult. But, first, we have to address incidents from your past that may have caused you to develop this alternative reality." She shook her head in confusion. "Dr. Green I just want to go home" "And you will, Moneca. You will." Moneca shook her head as she stood to her feet and walked out of his office. As she walked back to her room, she couldn't stop thinking about the information Dr. Green just told her. She felt as if the world was on her shoulders as she laid on her bed as she started to read the material he gave her and tried to make sense of her life. Sitting up as she held her head in her hand, she then looked up when she heard footsteps in the hall. Standing up, Moneca noticed it was Kina walking down the hall. "Hey, Moneca. Jackie is looking for you," Kina said as she walked into Moneca's room. "For what?" she asked. "She said that you have mail." Looking at Kina with a surprised look on her face, she placed her hand on her chest and asked, "Are you sure it's for me? I haven't received mail since I got to this place." "Yes, it's for you," she said as she then turned around. "As a matter of fact, there goes Jackie right there." Moneca watched as Jackie walked down the hall, towards her room with an envelope in her hand. When Jackie reached her room, she remained quiet as she tossed the envelope to Moneca and walked away. Looking down at the envelope, Moneca held it in her hand as she read who it was from. "Oh, my God," she said as tears started racing down her cheek.

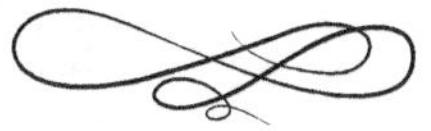

Chapter 11

OCEAN

This motherfucker, Dr. Green, was starting to get on my damn nerves. I've been running things for a very long time and I'll be damned if he thinks he can come in and start messing things up for me. You see, I am one of Moneca's other identities. I was created years ago, when that bitch-ass-nigga Rex had those guys come in and rape her. I took over Moneca's conscious because she wasn't strong enough to handle it. I had sex with all four of those men. Yes, Moneca was promiscuous back then, but she was still timid. I, on the other hand, was wild and crazy. I rode all those niggas like a cowgirl and even let two of them fuck me in the ass. So the fuck what! If you knew what I have been through then you wouldn't give a damn, either. It always brings me pleasure when my mind wanders back to the day I got my revenge on Rex. Shortly after I healed and was strong enough to get my revenge, I went back to his apartment and gave him what he deserved. There was no way I was going to let him get away with what he did to Moneca. Sure I couldn't track down all the assailants, but I knew where the main one laid his head at night. I bought a gun from a hustler. It didn't take much for me to sneak into Rex's apartment late one night to seek my revenge. I stood over his bed, smirking at him lying with that overgrown bitch Mona. I inserted the tip of my gun into her sleeping mouth. She quickly awoke and sat up in her bed. "Don't make a sound bitch," I said through clenched teeth. Her eyes widened with fear. "Bitch you got two seconds to get the fuck out of here," I said as I pulled the gun out of her mouth, but kept it pointed at her. She sat there with her body shaking uncontrollably as I started counting. "One . . ." I cocked my gun and the bitch could've qualified for the Olympics by the speed of her exit. She didn't bother to put on an inch of clothing as she rushed out the bedroom and front door naked as a newborn baby. I kicked the side of Rex's bed hard as hell with my foot. When he finally opened his eyes and rubbed them, the color drained from his face when he saw a gun pointed at him with my finger on the trigger. "What are you doing here?" he asked as held the palm of his hands out towards me like they could protect him. "That's the hand you beat me with," I simply said as I pulled the trigger. Boom! My aim was perfect. I smiled mischievously as the bullet entered his left hand and the sheets began to soak with his blood. "Argh!" he yelled as he then groaned in pain. As he tried to get out of his bed, I pointed the gun straight at his head. "Motherfucker if you make another move, I will blow your got damn brains out." "Moneca, baby, we can talk about this." he tried to reason. I stared into his eyes as I started to laugh. "Big, bad ass Rex. You don't look so tough now, do you?" "Moneca . . ." "Look, nigga. Moneca's not here, okay?" "What?" he asked with confusion. "You hurt her, Rex. You hurt her real bad. But it's all good because now I'm going to hurt you," I said with a demonic tone. "I didn't mean to hurt you, Moneca. Baby, I'm sorry!" he cried. "I said I'm not Moneca!" He quickly closed his mouth as he eyed the floor. "Rex, ya'll could've been good together. All you had to do was love her. But, you fucked up, nigga. And now you have to pay. She's going to have your baby and live happily ever after. There's no way I'm going to let you get away with what you did to her." He slowly stood to his feet, dressed in nothing but his Calvin Klein boxers as blood continued to ooze from his hand wound. I knew I didn't have much time as I was sure the neighbors had heard the gun shot and Mona probably went to go get help by now, too. "You let them niggas violate her, Rex. Then, you laughed at her and beat her ass as if she was nothing, but a piece of meat. So, now I'm going to hit you where it hurts," I said as I clenched my teeth and pulled the trigger to my gun, again. Boom! I shot him right in his testicles. He screamed out in pain as his balls exploded. I watched as he fell to the ground and yelled out in sheer agony. Tucking my gun in the back of my pants, I laughed as I then discreetly walked out of his bedroom and apartment. I was several blocks away from his apartment when I then heard sirens in the distance. Pulling my gun out of my back pants, I wiped it with the bottom of my shirt and tossed it in a nearby dumpster. I was then able to quietly leap back into bed with Fred. When he felt me tossing and turning, he woke up to make sure I was alright. I assured him that I was okay and watched as he drifted back off to sleep. Moneca was lucky to have him. They were getting married in the morning and she would leave town with him soon. Rex would never be able to retaliate. Even though I know I was wrong for doing some things without Moneca knowing, but as I really think about it, what the hell does Moneca need to know about me for? We have been doing just fine this far. I have saved her from a lot of heart ache and a lot of pain. I am strong enough to handle it for the both of us. I like to think of myself as a certified bitch. I just don't take no shit and that's all there is to it. I slipped up and accidentally revealed myself when I attacked Dr. Green, but I couldn't let him hurt Moneca by telling her what happened to her over the years. I just have to be more careful next time. I couldn't allow him to push my buttons. I have to admit, I would love to be released from this whack ass facility, but until Moneca tells them that her daughter is not real, these fools are not going to let her go. I couldn't do anything about that. Moneca truly believes that her daughter is out there and I couldn't make her forget her. In the meantime, though, I just live my life through her daughter, Oneca. Oneca gets on my damn nerves. I just don't have the patience for her timid ass. I try not to interfere when it comes to her, but she is just so boring. It started when she was eight-years-old. Her little weird ass was getting picked on at the playground and I was tired of the bullshit. I had to slap a few kids up before they realized they better stop fucking with her. I even had to cuss a few teachers out who I felt were being disrespectful. Oneca never really had a chance after I got through with people. I couldn't help it. She just let people walk all over her and I was not with that shit. When Oneca began to get abused, I again took over to protect her. I made sure she knew nothing of the abuse she sustained at the hands of the person she trusted. I could endure the pain that I knew that she could not. Although I couldn't stand that she does not have a back bone. I still feel that she deserves to be happy. The only way that she can do that is to not have to experience some of the realities of her life. I see myself as a stainless steel wall and there is nothing that can break me. Although I am here to protect them, I also like to have a little fun here and there. When Oneca was in college, I enjoyed my little fling with the Dean of Business. The sex was great and he gave me money whenever I needed it. He eventually fell in love and wanted more of me than I was willing to give. I described our relationship like exactly what it was; a fling. But, then he started talking about leaving his wife to be with me. I had to cut him off and cease all contact with him. He didn't like that and started fucking with me. He had the professors treating Oneca unfairly and not giving her the grades that she deserved. Shortly after, I stepped back in and showed up at his house threatening him and his wife with my .22mm and Oneca got expelled. Oops! I feel like Oneca bounced back well, though. She's happy at her boring little job, with her boring little friend, and her boring little life. Can you believe that this heifer is still a virgin? Well, technically she is not, but you know what I mean. I'm like what kind of twenty-five-year-old is walking around still a virgin? She needs to grow the hell up. I seriously would go crazy if I allow Oneca to run things. A strong knock at the door brought me out of my thoughts as I lounged on the couch. I got up and looked through the peep hole. I smirked as I recognized City's fine ass on the other side. I was only wearing a thong and a tank top. It didn't matter what I had on when it came to City. The only two things we ever discussed were money and fucking. Taking a deep breath as I opened the door, I smiled as he walked in and I immediately attacked him. Pressing my lips against his, I moaned as my tongue mingled with his. He kissed me back for a second before shoving me off of him. "I swear your ass is unstable," he said, taking a seat on the couch. "Why you say that baby?" I asked with my lips poked out. "Bitch, I see you in public and you act like you don't know me, but when we're behind closed doors, you act like I'm your man and fuck my brains out. What type of shit you on?" he asked, offensively. I laughed, "Did I hurt your feelings?" "Naw, never that. But what's up? You ashamed of a nigga or something?" I can't believe this thuggin' ass nigga is actually acting insecure. I thought to myself. I straddled him and said, "Never that, boo." I kissed his nose than licked his lips. "I just don't want anybody to get suspicious of what we got going on." "Yeah, I seen you with your little whack ass boyfriend," he said with a hint of anger in his voice. "What? You jealous?" I smiled. "Hell motherfucking naw," he quickly replied. "Of that nigga? Absolutely not." "So, what's the problem then?" "Nothing, I brought this information you needed." he said, shaking the envelope that he'd been holding, "It's all in here, names, addresses, banking information, social security numbers, and much more." "Good looking, boo. We gone make some serious paper off of this" "We sure are," he said with a smirk. "Money make me cum, mon-e-money make me cum," I started grinding on his dick as I sung Rick Ross's song. "You liked how daddy sucked that pussy the other night, didn't you?" he whispered into my ear. "Um-hmm, daddy," I said with my eyes closed still grinding on his growing dick. "Bitch, you pissed me off with that bullshit. Throwing me out the house and shit. What is with you and this innocent role you fall into?" he asked, his tone changing. I laughed as I said, "But, I brought yo ass back up in here and fucked you until you didn't have a drop of cum left up in that motherfucker. Didn't I?" He smirked, "I can't get enough of your crazy ass." I smiled as he inserted his finger into my pussy and slowly began to finger fuck me. "Oh, my God! Yes!" I shrieked. He held me as he stood to his feet, still moving his fingers in and out of me. I wrapped my arms around his neck and began to bounce up and down, riding his fingers. "Oh shit, City! Nigga, don't stop," I screamed. In one split second, he dropped his pants and inserted that hard dick into me. I cried out in pleasure as he got into rhythm. Our bodies rocked together as I fucked him harder; bouncing up and down on that dick while he stood there palming my ass. I could feel the pressure building as he kept hitting my G-spot over and over again. "Oh, shit! You feel so good, daddy!" I yelled out in pleasure. I came on that dick and he wasn't too far behind. I bit down on his shoulder as my body convulsed. We both then fell back on the couch and exhaled. I then opened my eyes as I tasted a salty substance in my mouth. "Did I draw blood?" I asked, laughing at his bleeding shoulder. He tossed my ass off the top of him and stood up while observing his shoulder. "Bitch, you are fucking crazy," he said as I watched him walk towards my bedroom then stop and look back at me. "Bring that ass in here for round two."

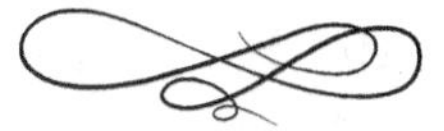

Chapter 12

ONECA

Work has been crazy for the past couple of weeks and I've been busier than ever. My corporate office is having me do an audit on all claims filed within the past six months, due to suspicion of fraud within one of the regional offices. I've been coming in on the weekends just to go through all of our computer files and paper files and match everything up. I've been even more upset that I haven't heard from my father since our little confrontation weeks ago at his house. I'm also very angry at him after reading the letter addressed to him from my mother. The letter revealed to me the exact opposite of what he has been telling me all of my life. I couldn't believe that for the past twenty-three-years my mother has been living in a psychiatric facility in Texas. Apparently, my father had her admitted and refuses to bring her home. It was very sad the way she begged him to come and get her and how she just wanted to be with me; her daughter. After reading the letter, I didn't know how to feel. I was happy to learn that I did have a mother that wanted to be in my life, but I was sad to see her beg my father to bring her home. I was hurt that she'd been away from me for all of these years, and I was angry at my father for lying to me all of these years. Even though I found out the real truth about my father, I just couldn't bring myself to confront him. I decided to take matters into my own hands and do some research of my own. I provided the information to Nate. I also called the facility, but of course, they couldn't release any real information. They stated that they couldn't confirm or deny that she was even a patient there. I was highly frustrated and came to the conclusion that I would have to travel to Texas myself in order to meet my mother face to face. Unfortunately, with everything going on at work, I wouldn't be able to take the time to make that drive until everything was sorted out. Sitting at my desk, I glanced across the street at The Bank of Colorado, wondering where Mikey had been lately. I hope he still wasn't uncomfortable about that condom he found on my bathroom sink. I had absolutely no idea where it came from and needed Mikey to support through all this madness in my life. We hadn't spoken since that day and I never had realized how much he really meant to me. After I continued to look outside, I suddenly noticed him coming out the bank. It was a windy day and he was zipping up his jacket while walking down the sidewalk. My mouth dropped in shock as I noticed him approach someone standing on the corner. City and Mikey exchanged a few words and Mikey handed City an envelope. City quickly slipped it into his jacket and continued on down the street. Mikey crossed the street, towards my office, and walked right up to my door. He suddenly made a sharp turn and continued to walk pass my window. He then glanced up at me and winked. I quickly looked down, not even realizing that he knew I was watching him. I didn't have time to process the encounter I had just seen between Mikey and City before the office phone began to ring. Taking a deep breath, I then answered the phone. "Oneca, this is Susan; you're District Manager." "Yes, Ma'am. What can I do for you?" "The District office has been able to target the specific time frame of the false claims that have been coming through your region. They have narrowed it down to either your office or the two Denver offices." "Okay," I said as I raised my eyebrow. "I need you to pull every claim dated from three weeks ago. They believe majority of these claims were filed during that time." "I will get right on it." "I will be coming to your office on Friday. I expect you to have everything pulled and ready for me." "Yes, Ma'am. I will have it all ready for you," I said before ending the call as I sighed in frustration. Her request would take me hours and there was no way I could finish it by Friday without staying late either today or tomorrow. I was really upset about her request since I was supposed to meet up with Nate to see if he had any new information for me. I was so anxious to see what he'd discovered so far. Pulling out my cell phone, I then scrolled down to his name and pressed the sent button and waited for him to answer. "Hi, Nate, this is Oneca Alvarez. I'm calling to cancel our appointment today. Unfortunately, I have to work late and won't have time to meet with you." "I'm sorry to hear that. I had some significant information to share with you." "I'm so mad. I wanted to me up with you today but there's no way I can make it." "Since you gave me your mother's information, I have made quite the discovery. Are you sure you can't squeeze me in?" "Only if you could come by my office later this evening," I said. "I could make that happen. I've discovered some very interesting information about your father, too." "My father?" "Yes, will seven 'o'clock work for you?" "That'll be perfect," I said as I thanked him and ended the call. I spent the next few hours going through insurance claims. I found it odd that there were several similar claims filed through my office over the past couple of weeks. They were primarily hit and runs and one person accidents, however; most of the insurance checks were mailed to the same P.O. Box. After digging a bit more, I found that I was the agent that handled these claims. It just didn't make sense to me. I didn't recognize any of the names on these claims and had no recollection of filing them. I suddenly realized I was going to be in serious trouble if I didn't figure all of this out soon. Time flew by as I gathered the information for these suspicious claims. I had collected eighteen by the time Nate knocked on my office door. I quickly rushed to the door to let him in. He greeted me and took a seat in one of the office chairs. "You look upset," he said. "It's just been a long day," I said, still trying to understand what I had recently discovered. "Fortunately, for you, I've been working hard on your case as well." "Great. I'm anxious to hear what you have discovered. Would you like some water?" "Sure, I'll take some." I stood to my feet, walked to a nearby corner when I had a small refrigerator, opened it up, and took out a bottle of water. Walking over to him, I then handed it to him and watched as he opened it. I then took a seat across from him, eager to hear the information he had for me. "Where do I start?" he asked himself before taking a deep breath. "Well, first of all, your mother is in fact residing in a psychiatric unit in Austin, Texas. Your father had her admitted there years ago. According to classified records, he had her admitted based off the fact that she believed she had a daughter." "Wait, what do you mean? I am her daughter." "Indeed you are, but, for some reason, your father reports that you were never born." "What the hell?" I said with pure shock and confusion. "I also have taken these pictures over the past few weeks. They include surveillance from your house, your job, and your father's house," he said as he handed me an envelope. I took the pictures out of the envelope and began to look through them. They included candid photos of me entering and leaving my apartment and job. There were also several photos of my dad working in his yard and running errands around Aurora. There were photos of me standing in my dad's yard talking to Mrs. Jones too. "Oneca, why didn't you tell me that you and Mikey were dating?" Nate asked. "We're not," I replied. "If you keep looking through those photos, you'll see photos of him leaving your apartment during late hours of the night. Most of the time it was usually three or four in the morning." "No, I don't know what you're talking about. Mikey has never been to my place that late," I replied before I flipped through several pictures of Mikey entering and leaving my apartment. The photos were dated from past two weeks. "Plus, I haven't even spoken to Mikey in the past two weeks." I said as I tilted my head and continued to skim through the pictures. "He was definitely at your place. Even this week he was there at least three times." "I just don't understand." "Does the name Isaac Jackson ring a bell?" Nate asked, changing the subject. "No," I said as I then squinted my eyes. "Wait, hold on a minute." Standing to my feet and walking over to my desk, I skim through a pile of folders I had on the back table and sure enough, there was a file with the name Isaac Jackson printed on it. "Who is he?" I asked, handing Nate the file. Nate picked the pictures up off the desk where I had laid them down and handed me several of them. "These are photos of him leaving your apartment, too. He's been there more than a few times." "City!" I exclaimed recognizing his face. Nate nodded, "His real name is Isaac Jackson." "Oh, my God. I'm so confused," I said as I held my head. "Tell me what you know about his guy?" "I don't really know him. He approached me one day while I was having lunch with Mikey. He kept calling me "O" and he acted as if we knew each other, but I have no idea who he is. Somehow he knew where I lived and showed up at my place that night. Like a fool, I let him in and we had a brief encounter before I put him out." "What kind of encounter?" Nate asked. "It's really embarrassing," I said as I took a deep breath and exhaled. "But, it was a sexual encounter." "Are you in a relationship with this guy?"

"No, I don't even know him." Nate stared at me skeptically. "So, I have evidence of two males entering and leaving your apartment frequently at all hours of the night, but you are not in a relationship with either of them?" "Nate I know it sounds crazy and skeptical, but his is why I hired you in the first place. My life doesn't make sense!" "Okay. I just don't understand why Mikey led you to me if he was more involved then he let on," Nate said as he scratched his head. I shrugged. "I thought Mikey was the one thing that did make sense in my life, but after what I saw today, I guess I can't say that anymore." "What happened today?" "I saw Mikey and City talking on the street corner and Mikey gave City an envelope." "Hmm, that's odd. Something is definitely up. From the looks of it, you are going to go down for insurance fraud if you don't get it figured out," he said, flipping through the file I had given him. "You have several claims filed by Isaac Jackson that doesn't appear legitimate. If anyone finds out that you have a personal relationship with him, you are definitely facing some criminal charges." "This can't be happening," I said in despair. "What did I ever do to deserve this?" "Oneca, I have no idea. But, the odds are definitely not in your favor. There are two more things I wanted to address with you that's about your father." "What is it?" "Do you recognize this man?" he asked as he took out another picture and handed it to me. The picture was of my father and another man standing on my father's porch. The expression on my father's face was obviously of anger. The other man was strikingly handsome. He appeared to be in his mid to late forties, he had smooth, dark skin, and a salt-and-pepper goatee. He was dressed in black slacks and a white silk shirt. He was leaning on a cane and look as if he was conversing with my father. Unlike my father's anger expression, the man appeared to be calm. "No, I don't recognize him. Who is he?" "I'm still working on figuring that out, but my instinct tells me that he will lead us to a break in this story. Whatever he and your father were discussing obviously had your father pissed off." "I can see that, too." "Which brings me to my last question, Moneca. Did you have any idea that there were allegations against your father years ago for statutory rape?" "Say what now?" I asked, snapping my neck back. "Your father should have been a registered sex offender when he was eighteen-years-old, but for some odd reason, there were never any charges filed against him." "What?" I exclaimed, "There's no way!" "Unfortunately, it's true," Nate said as he stood to his feet and gathered his photos. "Oneca I will be in touch." "Wait, you just can't drop that information on me like that and then just leave!" "Oneca, I have to get going if you want me to do my job, but listen to me when I say, you need to be very careful of the people that you are surrounding yourself with. At this point, you can't trust anyone." I just sat there silently as Nate made his way out of my office. Nate's words ran through my head. I just couldn't fathom my father being in trouble with the law. Is that why he left the military? How could I have grown up with him and not known any of this? Why didn't he want me to have anything to do with my mother? Who was the man in the picture with my father? Why did I feel such a strong connection to him? My ringing phone snapped me out of my thoughts. I stared the caller id as it displayed incoming call from Daddy. I stared at the phone until it stopped ringing. Nate's words just kept ringing in my head. "At this Point you can't trust anyone."

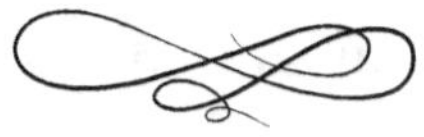

Chapter 13

MONECA

Moneca sat in awe as she stared at her mother who sat across from her in the visitation room. Looking at her mother, it wasn't the weak, depressed woman she remembered. Her mother looked healthy, vibrant, happy and most importantly, alive. "Hi, Monny!" her mother said, calling Moneca by her nickname. "Mama? Is that you?" she asked. "Yes. It's me, baby." Moneca sat there and looked at her mother. She had caramel, glowing skin, jet black hair that was pulled into a ponytail, and glistening, hazel eyes. There wasn't one wrinkle on her face. She wore a mint colored blouse and a pair of stone washed jeans. There was a single pearl in each of her ears. Her nails were French tipped and there was a shiny diamond ring on her left ring finger. Moneca's mother was sixty-three-years-old but looked twenty years younger. Moneca was in denial because the mother she remembered had ashy skin, dull hair, and a dull, dark look in her eyes. This was not the Wynita Robinson that she used to know so well. "Moneca, I know you are in disbelief," her mother, Wynita, said. "I don't even know what to say. You've changed." "I got better, honey." "Where have you been? "I got married twenty years ago and I've been living in Georgia" "Why didn't you reach out? Do you have any idea what I have been through?" "I had no idea. I thought you and Fred were living in bliss somewhere." "Fred is not the person we thought he was." "Moneca I had no idea. He was always so sweet. That's why when I finally learned where you were, I wrote you that letter." "I was so surprised to hear from you, that's why I asked you to come and visit me. I haven't seen anyone that I knew when I was younger for years." "I know, honey. You sounded so desperate and sad when you wrote back, I had to drop everything to come and see you. I'm so sorry that you had to go through this, Moneca. I had no idea," Wynita said sincerely. "You have got to get me out of here," Moneca said as tears formed in her eyes. "I'm going to do everything in my power to get you out. Ray and I . . ." "Who is Ray?" "He's my husband. He has been a life saver for me, Moneca. He is the reason that I am better." "Mama, what happened? How did you get better?" "When you and Fred moved away, things got worse for me." Moneca looked down in shame and said,

"Mama, I'm sorry. My intentions were to bring you with us, but I was going through so much during that time." "It's okay, Monny. You inherited some things from me that I should have prepared you for, but I never had the chance." "I'm worried about my daughter, mom." "I'll do everything I can to help you get to her," her mother said, causing Moneca to look up at her in shock. "So you believe me I say I have a daughter?" "Of course, why wouldn't I? You're my daughter. I know when you're lying and when you're telling the truth." Moneca smiled through her teary eyes. She didn't know how to handle that the fact that after all these years, someone finally believed that she had a daughter. "Moneca, I'm sorry I wasn't there for you after your father left and that I wasn't there after all of these years," her mother said as she held her head low in shame. "It's okay, Mama. I understand, believe me. I mean, look where I am," she said as she waved her hand around the visitation room. Wynita nodded and said, "I don't know why they're holding you against your will, but believe me when I say, I'll get to the bottom of it." "Okay, I know you will, mom. You have to tell me how you got better." "Ray, my husband, was an angel sent from God. Shortly after you and Fred moved away. Apparently, I was aimlessly wandering the streets when Ray discovered me and took me to a hospital. He stayed by my side and we eventually fell in love. He is a little younger than me though, but I love him so much. I've been on my meds and I attended counseling. I'm okay, Monny. And, you can be, too." "I am so glad to hear that. I can't wait for you to get me out of here. I never thought it would happen. I thought all hope was gone." They both continued to chat and reminisce until their visitation time ran out. After visitation ended, her mother left promising that she would return shortly. Moneca was so happy to the point that she couldn't contain herself. She couldn't believe how her life was slowly but surely changing, in just a short period of time. Weeks ago, she had no hope that she would ever get out. But now, she was willing to tell those people that her daughter didn't exist and make one last attempt to do it. Even though she was convinced and feeling good that she was getting out soon, she still believe that Dr. Green trying to convince her that she had multiple personality disorder was absurd. She'd been avoiding her sessions with him for that very reason. Moneca wasn't trying to spend any more time hearing something that she knew wasn't true about. To avoid his sessions, she been telling the nurses that she was sick, but she knew it wouldn't last long. Now that she was sure that her mother would get her out of that facility, she really cared less about avoiding Dr. Green. Moneca was just ready to leave that place and to never look back.

When she arrived back to her room after her visit with her mother, Nurse Jackie informed her that she wouldn't be able to miss another appointment with Dr. Green. Nurse Jackie practically dragged her down the hall, towards his office. "You fools are the same," she huffed and puffed as she pulled Moneca by the arm. Moneca remained quiet the whole walk. When they reached Dr. Green's office, Nurse Jackie knocked on the door and opened it. "Here is your next appointment," she smiled as she then pushed Moneca into the room. "Bitch," Moneca mumbled as she then turned around and looked at Dr. Green He smiled and said, "Moneca, have a seat." She sat down across from his desk, wondering if he already knew about her visit with her mother. "Moneca, we have so much work to do. Why have you been missing our sessions?" "I'm just . . . I mean . . . I don't think that . . ." her words fumbled out as she tried to come up with an explanation. "Does this have anything to do with our last session and my thoughts on your mental state?" he asked with his eyebrows raised. "It has everything to do with it," she finally admitted. "And does this have anything to do with your visit this morning?" "How did you know about that?" "Moneca, you live in a Psychiatric Facility. Everything that occurs in here is monitored." "Well, then you should know that I won't be here much longer." "I know that your mother has already contacted our legal representative and has demanded your release." "So what's the problem?" she asked, standing to her feet in anger. "Moneca, please sit down and remain calm. It's not that simple. Fred Alvarez has documents declaring him as your power of attorney for all medical decisions. You were declared incompetent years ago." "I would never sign anything giving that power to Fred. My mother is my next of kin and she can make those decisions!" "That may be true, but it will take our legal officers to determine that. Plus, at the time, your mother was incompetent too." "Even if he claims that this is true, she is better now. He can just sign over those rights to my mother. Why would he want to be bothered with me, anyway? He's forced me to stay here for twenty-three-years!" Dr. Green shrugged, "I don't know if it's that simple." "You people are crazy. I have never in my life heard such bullshit. I will get out of here, and my mother will make sure of it." "That may be true, Moneca. And if it does happens, that means we don't have very much time." "Time for what?" "For your identities to reveal themselves and to rejoin as one." "Dr. Green you have got to be kidding me, right?" "No, I'm not. I take your progress in my sessions very seriously." "I'm starting to believe that you may need to be the one receiving treatments," Moneca said seriously. She watched as Dr. Green pulled out her diaries from his desk and asked,

"Moneca can we talk about your entries?" She nodded. "You have several entries as yourself, but there are also several entries from Oneca." "What?" "Moneca, you are the only one who has had access to these journals. Can you explain how there are entries from you, as well as Oneca?" Dr. Green asked as he handed Moneca her diary. She quickly glanced at the pages that Dr. Green had marked. There were several entries from her daughter, Oneca. "Maybe I missed her so much that I wrote from her point of view," she said with a shoulder shrug. "I don't know." "These entries are very detailed. There's even an entry stating that you believe you may be in trouble with the law?" "Dr. Green, I don't know," she said with frustration. "This is just pen and paper. I can write whatever I want! Oneca is real and I will return to her." "I believe Oneca is one of the identities that your conscious has created. She was never born, Moneca."

Chapter 14

OCEAN

"**F**uck you, Dr. Green!" I yelled at him. "M-m-moneca?" he stammered as his eyes widened in shock. I smiled at him as I began to pace around his office. "Oneca?" I stopped pacing, stared into his eyes, and with the fakest, helpless voice I can muster up, I said, "Dr. Green, you have to help me get to my daughter!" "Are you Moneca or are you someone else?" he asked, skeptically. He didn't buy it. He was smarter than I thought. "I got to go, now. Maybe we will meet again," I said as I started to walk out of his office. "Moneca, wait!" I heard him yell as I ran out of his office and down the hall. Turning around, I could see Nurse Jackie running straight for me. "Where the hell do you think you're going?" she yelled. I cut my eyes at her and gave her a sinister glare as I passed right by her. She was so taken aback by the venom in my expression that she quickly lost that smart mouth of hers. She stood still as

123

I continued on down the hallway. I had decided that I had enough of this place. I made my way to the exit door. Reaching behind the counter at the empty nurse's station. I pressed the release button that subsequently opened the double doors. I was halfway down the corridor before I heard the sirens go off. I could see sunlight through the second set of double doors. I briskly walked headed for the outside world. I began to hear footsteps rushing behind me. I silently convinced myself that if I could make it through those doors then I would be free. Three quick steps and my hands gripped the door handle. I smiled as my freedom was within reach. I suddenly felt a sharp pinch in my neck, but I didn't stop. I continued through the doors and started to make my way to the parking lot. Before I could make it to the parking lot, I felt another sharp pinch in my neck before my body became weak and fell to the ground. That was the last thing I remembered before everything went black. "Moneca, wake up. It's time for your meds," a nurse said, waking me out of my sleep. I opened my eyes and stared up at the nurse in confusion. "What the hell?" I groaned as I grabbed the back of my head that was throbbing with pain. "I know you are probably confused, honey. You've been asleep for twelve hours." "Why does my head hurt?" "You had a pretty bad fall in our parking lot. What were you thinking? You can't just walk out of here like that, Moneca. You've been here long enough to know that." "Did I get sedated?" "Yes," she replied sympathetically. I tried to lift my arms but couldn't. "What the hell?" I shrieked as I noticed my arms and legs were tied down. "I don't need to be restrained! Untie me!" "Dr. Green will have to determine that, Moneca. He will come and evaluate you as soon as he comes in to work this morning. You are considered a flight risk." "Fuck this shit," I yelled as I struggled against the restraints. "Moneca, I've never seen you behave this way." "Well get used to it bitch!" I sneered at her. She just shook her head as she forced my mouth open with one hand and forced several pills into my mouth before pouring water into my mouth. I tried to spit them out, but couldn't. One angry tear rolled from my eye as I stared at the ceiling. Weakness was not a character of mine. Weakness was a part of Moneca and Oneca, but not me. Hours later, Dr. Green entered my room. I looked up at him as he came and stood over me. I could see in his eyes that he was pleased that I was helpless. I wanted to snatch his eyebrows off of his face. "Who are you today?" he asked, feigning sincerity. "Who do you want me to be?" I asked, mockingly. "Why does this have to be difficult? I just want to help you." "Yeah right," I said through pursed lips. "I have spoken to your mother," he said. "And?" I asked nonchalantly. "If you agree to one final intensive session then I will consider signing your release papers." "I aint doing shit" "Why are you so resistant? Who are you?" "What about Fred?" I ignored his question. "I am the head psychiatrist in this facility and if I determine that there is no medical reason for you remain in this facility, then you will be released." "Dr. Green, don't fuck with me." "I want to arrange one final session; an intervention per say." "What good will it do?" "It will help you to reveal, recognize, and rejoin your multiple identities." "I've already told you, I don't have other identities. I'm not doing that bullshit!" "If you refuse, then we won't have no choice, but to deny your mother's request to release you." "Fuck you and this motherfucking hospital! You can't hold me here!" "We have and we will. We've done it for twenty-three years." Dr. Green stated matter-of-factly, before turning to leave the room. I'm not sure what Dr. Green has in mind, but I knew I don't like the sounds of it. I've been running things for a long time and I refuse to allow him come in and mess things up. I just felt so exhausted. I just want to close my eyes and rest. I feel like I just need to rest for a little while and after I wake up, I will figure out how to get myself out of here. Moneca: "Dr. Green what are you doing in here?" Moneca asked as she noticed him leaving her room. He turned around, starring at her in bewilderment. "I came here to talk to you." "About what? Why am I being restrained?" "What is the last thing that you remember?" he asked, walking towards my bed. "I remember you showing me diary entries and saying that I was writing from my daughter's point of view." "You don't recall anything after that?" "No. What happened to me? My head is killing me," she winced in pain as she sat her head up. "You tried to escape." "I did what?" she asked in shock. Looking down at her, Dr. Green then asked, "Moneca, do you want to go home?" "More than anything." "Will you agree to an intensive session with me?" "If it will get me out of here." "All I ask is that you fully commit and participate. It will involve your mother and other people from your past." "Like who?" "Your husband and anyone else who had a significant impact on your mental state." "Oh, I definitely want to confront Fred." "I will get everything arranged. I will get the nurses to take those restraints off of you, too. I don't think we'll have any more trouble for the time being." "Thank you, Dr. Green," she said as she watched him walk out of her room.

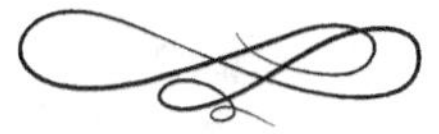

Chapter 15

ONECA

I'd been avoiding everyone since my meeting with Nate. I just didn't know where to start when it came to rationalizing the information that was given to me. My Regional Director did show up and it did not take her long to realize that my name was on majority of the fraudulent claims. I knew pleading with her and trying to convince her that I had no idea what was going on was pointless. I just packed up all my belongings and walked out of the office. I knew it was a small chance that she would believe that I've been going through this my whole life. Would she really believe my history of being involved in events that I had no had no idea I was actually involved in? I just hoped that charges were not brought against me. The crazy thing was, I had no idea where the money was or who really was behind the whole scheme. I'd been spending majority of my time inside my home depressed and distant from the world. I had no one to turn to, at al. I just couldn't bring myself to answer my father or Mikey's calls. I felt completely alone in the world. I finally decided that the only person who could help me make sense of my life was my mother. With that thought, I've decided to pack some clothes and head to Austin, Texas. The ringing phone caused me to stop packing my things for a moment as I then answered my phone. "Hello?" "O, this is City." "What do you want, Isaac?" I spat. "What's with the animosity shorty? We're in some deep shit." "Yeah, I guess your little get rich quick scheme didn't work, huh?" "What do you mean my plan? This whole thing was your damn idea! Yo, I swear to God, if you try to fuck me over, I will kill you my damn self!" "Listen, I didn't have anything to do with it or you! I don't know how you were able to get my name on those documents, but I swear, I will get to the bottom of it." I could hear him take a deep breath before he said, "Look, Ocean, this is not the time for games." "Ocean? Who in the hell is Ocean?" "Baby, listen, I saw the police leaving my house an hour ago. Do you have any idea why they would be looking for me?" "Yes, because Expedite Insurance gave them your name, along with mine." "Why didn't you warn my ass?" "Saving your ass is not at the top of my list right now."

"Ocean, please . . ." "Who the hell is Ocean?" I exclaimed. "My name is Oneca!" "Oneca? What?" he asked with confusion. "City, where is the money?" I asked, calming my voice down. "I have my share just like you have yours." "Do you know what I did with mine?" "No, baby girl. What is really going on?" "I really don't know what's going on. I don't know how you think you know me, I just don't know!" "I'm getting ready to come over there." "Why?" "Because, I can't go back to my place! We need to sit down and figure this shit out. And, I'm not gone let you play the innocent role." "I'm getting ready to go out of state." "What the fuck? So you was just gone leave my ass high and dry huh?" he yelled. "Me leaving has nothing to do with you!" "Look, just stay put, okay? I'm ten minutes away," he said before ending the call. I didn't care what City said. I didn't need him coming over here trying to pull me into his drama. What I did know was that I needed to get to Austin sooner rather than later. Just as I started to pull my suitcase out of my bedroom to the living room, I got a knock on my door. I quickly rushed to the door, ready to let City have it, but to my surprise, there were two male detectives standing before me, both flashing their badges. "Good Afternoon, Ma'am. My name is Lieutenant Allen Fipps and this is Detective Bron Perry. Are you Oneca Alvarez?" I nodded my head as I looked at them with caution. Lt. Fipps quickly pulled out a pair of handcuffs, "Oneca Alvarez you are under arrest for fraud and embezzlement of funds in connection with Expedite Insurance, anything you say can and will be used against you in a court of law. You have the right to an attorney. If you cannot afford an attorney, one will be appointed to you. Do you understand the rights I have just read to you?" "Wait a minute!" I panicked as he forced the cuffs on me. "You got the wrong person, I had nothing to do with it!" "Ma'am, if you can't afford an attorney, one will be appointed to you," he repeated. "Isaac Jackson! You want Isaac Jackson!" I cried. "If you just wait a few minutes, he is on his way here." "Ma'am, we've already apprehended Mr. Jackson outside of your building just a few minutes ago. The gig is up," he said eyeing my suitcases that set on the floor. I cried as they led me out of my apartment, downstairs, and into their vehicle. I stared out the window as they drove me downtown to the police station. I saw no way of getting out of this one. I had seen the claims myself, with my name as the agent listed. How could I explain that I had absolutely no idea how my name got on those claims? Once I was processed and booked in, they left me sitting a room for hours. I'd been crying nonstop. Lt. Fipps eventually entered the room and took a seat across from me at the table. My hands were handcuffed and resting in my lap. I was dressed in a jail issued jumpsuit. "How are you today?" he asked, like he hadn't arrested me hours before and left me sitting in this cold ass room crying. "I've had better days." "Ms. Alvarez, why don't you tell me what happened?" "I don't know." I shrugged, helplessly. "So you don't know how over twenty thousand dollars in false auto insurance claims were processed through your office?" "Twenty thousand dollars? Are you serious?" "Why did you do it, Ms. Alvarez?" "I didn't do it, I swear!" I pleaded, as tears began to fall again. "Ms. Alvarez, you and your little boyfriend are going to do some serious time. The fact that we caught you attempting to leave town doesn't help, either." "I swear, I didn't do it!" I said as I dropped my head in shame. "Your Regional Manager spoke so highly of you, Oneca. Why did you do it, Ms. Alvarez? Did Mr. Jackson force you into his scheme?" I remained quiet as I continued to cry. "Mr. Jackson is a known hustler and con artist. We've had our eyes on him for a while. How did you get involved with him?" I just shrugged my shoulders and tried to wipe the tears from my face with my bounded hands. "Can I make a phone call?" I asked, desperately. "Ms. Alvarez, did Isaac Jackson better known as City, threaten you in any way if you did not cooperate with his plan?" he asked as he ignored my question. I was starting to catch on to what the Lieutenant was getting at. "What if he did?" "Your time can be greatly reduced. You may even be able to get a slap on the wrist. Maybe even just a few years of probation." At that point, I knew what I had to do. "Yes, he did. He said he would hurt me and my family if I didn't do what he said. I was scared," I said as tears of hurt and guilt flowed down my face. "Would you be able to testify that in a court of law?" I nodded my head. "Great," Lt. Fipps stood up, "Now, let's get you that phone call." I then stood to my feet as the two detectives led me out of the room and towards the pay phone. I watched as they then took the hand cuffs off of me as I then dialed Mikey's number. He answered on the first ring. "Mikey, I'm in trouble." "Oneca? Why are you calling from downtown?" "I'm in jail." "What! What happened?" he yelled. I had never heard Mikey raise his voice. "I'll explain all of that later. They arrested me for fraud and embezzlement, though." "Did you call your father?" "No, I don't want to talk to him." I snapped. "Oneca, you need to call your father." "No, Mikey! I can't face him right now." "Oneca, listen to me, your father can help you! Trust me!" "Mikey, get me out of here, please!" I begged. "I'm on my way." Several hours later, I was released. Mikey and my father were both waiting for me. I couldn't help it, I ran into the arms of my daddy. He hugged me so tightly. "Daddy, I didn't do it," I cried. "I know, baby," he rubbed my back, "The charges will be dropped." "What?" I looked up at him in confusion. "Baby, your mental health status is unstable. I highly doubt you will go to trial. But, if you do, you will have to plead insanity." "What are you talking about?" I was utterly confused. "Oneca, baby girl, you have Schizophrenia and that damn thug you were running around with took advantage of that." "I have what?!" I shouted. Mikey came over to me, took my hand, and said, "Oneca, calm down." "Mikey, why isn't this shocking news to you?" I exclaimed. He held his head down in shame. I snatched my hand from his. "You knew about this? This is some bullshit! I'm not crazy. Why are you saying this? Is this just a way to get me out of trouble? If it is, I'll go along with it! But don't be making up lies!" My daddy shook his head. "No, baby girl. What I am saying is true. I had to bring your Medical records down here so that you could be released. Let's go home so we can talk about it." I looked at him with shock as I backed away from the both of them. Mikey spoke up and said, "Oneca, City reported to the police that you were the brains behind the operation, but he kept referring to you as Ocean. Apparently, City had a relationship with you, but it wasn't really you." "Oneca, let's go home," my daddy intervened. "Stay away from me! You are a liar! I know all about my mother! You have been lying to me my whole life. It's because of you that I don't know her! I know everything daddy!" His eyes widened in surprise, "Oneca, honey . . ." "No, daddy, save it!" I shouted as I then turned and rushed out of the police station.

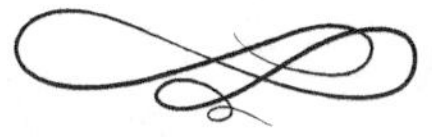

Chapter 16

MONECA

Moneca sat in her favorite chair across from Dr. Green's desk. She was completely nervous, fumbling her fingers together as she took a deep breath. Today was the day of her final session. She anticipated finally being released from that psychiatric facility after twenty-three-years. Her mother, Wynita, sat in the chair next to her, holding her hand and assuring her that everything would be alright. Dr. Green had her included in Moneca's treatment because he felt as if she was significant impact on Moneca's life. "How do you feel, Moneca?" Dr. Green asked. "I feel nervous, Dr. Green," she replied. "Why are you feeling nervous?" "I'm just nervous about everything. I'm ready to rejoin the real world. I'm happy my mother is here, though. It's just so many emotions running through me right now." Dr. Green smiled and said, "I'm so glad that you have made it to this point. I feel like today is the first day of the rest of your life." My mother cleared her throat and said, "Dr. Green, we're putting our trust in you to help my daughter. I want you to know that regardless of what occurs in this session, if she doesn't get out, I won't stop until I get out of here." Dr. Green nodded. "I understand that," He said as he turned to Moneca. "Did you read the material that I gave you on Schizophrenia?" "Yes, I did." "Do you have any questions about this disorder?" "I just can't get over the fact that you think I have another identity." "I think you have two alternative identities, your daughter being one of them. I have read your diary and you made several entries over the years, but what's constant is that you always write from in three different point of views." "Dr. Green, if my daughter says that she has a daughter, than I believe her." Wynita said. "But there is no proof that . . ." Dr. Green said but was interrupted by his ringing phone. "Dr. Green's office. Okay, great. I will have you send him in my office in just a moment," he said before ending the call. "Moneca, I need to make it clear to you that today will not be easy. We will talk about things that will be difficult for you to discuss. In most cases, Schizophrenia is caused by a traumatic event in someone's life. So traumatic that they can't deal with the memory, so they suppress it. You are more prone to develop schizophrenia if there is a history of mental health disorders in your family." "I have struggled with depression and anxiety my whole life," Wynita said. "Am I the cause of all her suffering?""Mental disorders can be treated and a person can live a completely normal life. I believe something happened in Moneca's life that has caused her to develop this disorder. Wynita started to cry. "But, I wasn't there for her, after my husband left. I just couldn't deal with life. She was just a little girl but she had to grow up fast. She was forced to take care of herself and me." "Mama, don't cry," Moneca comforted her. "It's okay." "No, it's not okay, you should not have had to grow up so fast." I just looked at Dr. Green helplessly as I tried to console my mother. "Ladies I prefer to utilize the Solution Focused Theory during my sessions. That means we focus on the solutions to our problems and we place all of our energy into making things right. There is no way to change the past, it happened and it's over. The only way to begin this road to recovery is stop wasting so much time being focused on the negative things from our past. Today's session will be beneficial because it will allow Moneca to have everything laid out on the table. She can process and it and hopefully, she can move on." Moneca and Wynita nodded in agreement. "Now, I have someone waiting to join us. He being here will mark the beginning of an emotional journey. Remember, no matter what happens, don't be afraid to express yourself.

But, you must remain in your seat and you must not become physically violent towards anyone." Dr. Green watched as Moneca nodded before he picked up his phone to call his secretary. "Can you have Mr. Alvarez to come on in?" Moneca's eyes darted between Dr. Green and Fred when he entered the room. Her heart slammed into her chest as her palms became sweaty. She watched as he took a seat before she harshly bit down on her bottom lip. "Hello, Fred," Wynita said with a voice laced with hatred. Fred nodded towards her with a nervous expression on his face. Moneca couldn't take her eyes off of him. She hadn't seen her husband in years. He'd aged nicely with his salt-and-pepper silky, short hair, and masculine built. He was dressed in a pair of black slacks and a gray Polo shirt. When Moneca kept staring a hole through him, Fred looked away. "Welcome, Fred," Dr. Green said. "As you know, you and I have spoken on the telephone several times about your wife, Moneca. And I am pleased that we are able to have this meeting today." "I just want to help her," he stated, nonchalantly. Dr. Greene turned to Moneca and said, "Moneca, I know you have several things that you want to say to your husband, but I'm going to allow him to speak first." Moneca wanted to protest, but with the stern look on Dr. Green's face, she kept quiet. Dr. Green turned back to Fred and said, "Fred, why don't you start with when you and Moneca first began as a couple." Fred finally made eye contact with her as he relaxed a bit and leaned back in his chair. Clearing his throat, he began. "I always cared for Moneca. We lived next door to each other most of our lives. We were friends as children, but as we got older, she became popular, and I was just a lonely nerd. When we were teenagers, Moneca began dating this guy named Rex. He was bad news and everybody knew it. But, she was head over heels for him. Anyway, one day just as I came home, I noticed Moneca lying on her porch outside of her door. I quickly ran to her and helped her inside her house. She had been beaten up pretty badly. She admitted that Rex had beaten her up. Once we got to the hospital, I also learned that she had been gang raped just weeks before, and Rex was behind it all. Apparently, he was some kind of pimp in our neighborhood." Moneca's eyes widened in sheer horror as the memories slowly started to come back to her. She felt like she was frozen in place; she couldn't move one single muscle. We then found out she was pregnant. Moneca insisted that it was Rex's baby. I didn't care about what happened to her, I just wanted to be with her. I wanted us to raise the baby together. I joined the Air Force and I asked Moneca to marry me. I was so angry at Rex for what he did to her that I wanted revenge. I showed up at his apartment one day and we got into a fight. I was no fighter by any means, but the anger took over me when he laughed in my face and called her a whore. I ended up whooping his ass. I messed him up pretty bad too. All I know is when I came to my senses, I was holding a lamp in my hands and Rex was lying on the floor with blood everywhere. I quickly left the scene and returned to Moneca's home. I never spoke a word of that day, until now," he paused and shuttered at the words he spoke. He then looked at Moneca and continued. "Monica lost the baby shortly after we got married. She never was the same after that. I think after what happened to her, she had put all of her happiness into that unborn child. When that baby didn't make it, she just could not handle it. I tried everything to get her back, but she was never the same. I hated to leave her, but I had to report to Basic Training." Looking at Fred in confusion, Moneca asked, "I lost my baby?" Fred nodded, "I just didn't know how to help you." Wynita held her daughter's hand as she cried. "Fred, go ahead and continue," Dr. Green said, softly. "When I returned from BMT, I was shocked to find Moneca pregnant again. Moneca had no recollection of losing the first baby, but I knew something wasn't right. When we went to the doctor, we learned that she was six weeks pregnant. We definitely hadn't had sex the weeks before I left for BMT, and I had been gone for eight weeks."

Fred suddenly became very uncomfortable as he shifted in his seat. He glanced out the window as he recalled their history. "I was distraught because I thought she had cheated on me. That night, I got drunk to drown my sorrows. I'd found a six pack my dad had stashed in the refrigerator. After finishing it, I went the store to get another. I became angry at the store clerk when he wouldn't sell to me because of my age. This girl approached me in the store. She was very attractive. She tried to calm me down and told me I could come back to her place where she had some beer. I followed her home. She was all over me as soon as we entered her place. We drank a couple of beers together and ended up having sex," Fred hung his head in shame. "What?" Moneca gritted in anger. "You cheated on me? How could you?" "Moneca it was all a set up!" he pleaded, "I later learned that Rex had sent the girl to seduce me. He showed up to my house the next day, threatening me. The girl was only sixteen-years-old and he claimed that he had it on video. She was saying that I raped her and he would turn me into the police if I didn't do what he said. This was all about revenge for him. He was walking on a cane, and I just regretted that I'd hurt him so badly because he held my future in his hands. He kept saying he was going to pay the both of us back for what we did to him. He kept calling you crazy. I just regretted that I ever went to his house. I felt like it was my entire fault." "What the hell, Fred? You've been keeping this a secret all these years?" Moneca shouted. "Moneca, he admitted that while I was gone, he had one of his goons break into your house and rape you. That's how you became pregnant again. I felt so guilty because the only reason I slept with that girl was because I thought you cheated on me. I knew my military career would be over if he went to the police, so I agreed to whatever he wanted." She shook her head in disbelief as a stream of tears cascaded down her cheek. How could all of these things had happened to me and I had no memory of it? "What did Rex want you to do, Fred?" Dr. Green asked. "Initially, he just told me to stay married to Moneca and raise the baby as my own. I had no problem with that. We left Oklahoma shortly after and moved on base at Buckley in Colorado. Moneca had a daughter and I loved her like my own. We named her Oneca Cheyenne Alvarez. Everything was fine for about two years. I didn't hear a word from Rex. Then, all of a sudden, one day he showed up at our doorstep demanding to take my daughter. There was no way I was going to let him take Oneca. He said the only way he would leave us alone was if I got rid of Moneca." "He wanted you to kill me?" she asked. Fred shook his head and said, "He forced me to have you committed." Her mouth dropped in shock as his words hit her like a ton of bricks. Her head throbbed with pain as the harsh thought of Rex being the reason that she'd been locked away for twenty-three-years.

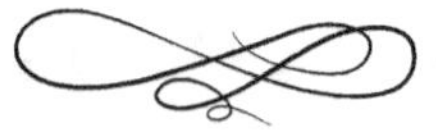

Chapter 17

OCEAN

Beads of sweat began to form on my forehead as I chased Moneca's husband around the room. He had a look of pure fear on his face as he ran from one side of the room to the other. I wanted to kill him. He attempted to slow me down by knocking down one of the chairs that sat in the office, but I quickly leaped over it and gripped the tail end of his shirt in my hand. I leaped onto his back and held on as he then began to spin around. "Ocean! Ocean!" I could hear someone calling for me to stop my attack, but at that moment, blinded by rage, I didn't care; I wanted blood. I began beating him on the top of his head as I then yelled, "I hate you! Die! Just die!" I was trying to pry my legs from around him while dodging my fists. He began to ram us both into the wall in hopes of making me fall, but I wanted him to suffer. I was relentless. I could feel someone trying to pull me off of him, but with the anger

I was feeling inside, I wasn't letting up. He was the reason for all my suffering; for all my pain. After a few more tugging on my back, Dr. Green was finally able to pull me off and we both tumbled to the ground. I started swinging and yelling trying to get up and go after him again. Moneca's husband stood to his feet and raced to the other side of the room. His chest heaved up and down as he stared at me with fear in his eyes. "You have got to calm down," Dr. Green said calmly in a soothing voice as I slowly gained my composure. "Dr. Green I hate him," I cried, internally fighting with myself for showing emotion. I'd held all this emotion inside for decades and hated that I appeared so vulnerable. No one was supposed to see this side of me. This side of me was not supposed to exist. "Remember we talked about expressing ourselves through words, you have got to let go of all of this anger." I slowly got up off of the floor and sat in one of Dr. Green's office chairs. Dr. Green went back to his desk and sat down. "I'm sorry," Moneca's husband stated, still apprehensive. I didn't even bother to look at him. I was upset with Dr. Green as well. How dare this mother fucker! Over the past years, Moneca had been meeting with him for many therapy sessions and had placed a lot of trust in him. She had confided in him about all of her struggles and how this man had betrayed her. I would have never agreed to this meeting.

Dr. Green was wrong for this; I protected Moneca all of this time. I kept things in order. She trusted Dr. Green, but I didn't. I had allowed her to form a bond with him and he was out of line! "What is your name?" Dr. Green asked me. What is wrong with this fool? He knows who I am. I heard him call my name earlier. "What is your name?" he asked again. A sly smile crept across my face as I leaned back in my chair and crossed my legs. "Dr. Green you know who I am," I said, barely controlling my sinister grin. "Tell me who you are," he said as he motioned his hand towards Moneca's husband, "Tell us who you are." I paused for a moment then sat up in my chair staring Dr. Green directly into his eyes, "Ocean, mother fucker. Ocean mother-fucking Robinson." A gasp was heard come from the corner where my previous victim was standing. Dr. Green smiled, "Nice to finally meet you." I didn't respond, but only turned and glared at the man I wanted to kill. I hated him with every fiber in my body. He looked at me with sad eyes of recognition. "Ocean," Dr. Green brought my attention back to him, "Why do you hate him? "He is evil, Dr. Green. You don't know the things he has done to me. He caused Moneca so much pain. He is sick and twisted!" He turned to him, "Is this true?" He shook his head and said, "I would never do that. I love Moneca." "Liar!" I yelled, jumping up from my chair and making my way towards him.

"Ocean!" Dr. Green called my name to stop me. "Ocean, I called this meeting today to help you. I want to help you confront your past. Moneca's husband is not your enemy, Ocean." I stared straight into Dr. Green's eyes trying to understand what he was telling me. "I have someone else from your past that you need to confront." I braced myself for the worst, knowing just forty-five minutes earlier Dr. Green just had Moneca's husband confront me. I watched as he picked up his phone, alerting his secretary that it was okay to allow the unknown person to enter. I turned towards the door, awaiting the stranger's arrival. "You've got to control yourself," Dr. Green said. I turned to question him and heard the door open from behind me. Turning around, I laid my eyes on the man I thought I would never see again, the man I thought I got rid of so many years ago, the man who caused me so much hurt and pain, and the man who tried to kill me. I was blinded by fury as I grabbed the letter opener off of Dr. Green's desk and raced towards the man as he had already shut the door and entered the room. He stood there leaning on his walking cane, but the look in his eye displayed confusion, he didn't know if he should try to rush back out the door or go toe to toe with me. By the time he made a decision, it was too late. "Calm down!" he shouted, holding his hands up in a defensive manner, but I could see the treacherous smirk on his face. "Fuck you, you evil ass bastard! I hate you!" I yelled as I quickly grabbed a hold of him, pulled my arm back with so much force, and brought it forward, connecting the letter opener with his flesh. "Ocean, no!" I heard my mother yell, but it was too late. I had completely forgotten that she was in the room. I was shocked that she called out my name and not Moneca's. I looked down as I was on top of Rex. I saw that I had not actually stabbed him, but instead, I had missed his leg by an inch. He was on the ground, under me, trying to get me off of him. Two attendants quickly rushed into the room, grabbed me, and pulled me off of him. "Wait, don't hurt her," my mother pleaded. No one had ever pleaded for me before. I was supposed to be invisible. And how did she know my name? I thought to myself. "Ray, what are you doing here?" I heard my mother say as she looked at Rex. One of the attendants immediately motioned to inject me with a syringe. "Wait," Dr. Green called out, "She's calm. Don't inject her. She is calm; she didn't hurt him." The attendants were reluctant, but they eventually released their grip on me. I just stood there next to my mother. I watched as Rex reached for his cane and slowly stood to his feet. "What happened to you? Why are you walking with a cane?" I asked. "You did this, you little bitch," he spat with venom. "You broke into my house and you shot me in my nuts. The bullet went through my dick and my leg. I could never fuck again and I walk with a permanent limp." If looks could kill, I would have died on the spot from the anger in Rex's eyes. "Wait a minute," my mother stated, "What the fuck is going on? Ray how do you know my daughter?" "I need everyone to take a seat," Dr. Green tried to interject. Everyone was standing around and too amped to take a seat. Fred spoke up from the back of the room, "Wynita, this man is not who you think he is. This is Rex; the man who hurt your daughter." "What the fuck?" my mother shouted, "I've been married to you for twenty years!" "Look, Wynita, this had nothing to do with you, okay? You just happened to be the mother of this little bitch." "What the fuck you mean this doesn't have anything to do with me? You fucking married me as part of a plan to seek revenge on my daughter? You trifling mother fucker! You mean to tell me the reason why you got a midget dick and we never could fully fuck was because my daughter shot you in the dick?" she shouted. I laughed hysterically at my mother's words. I felt bad that she had been used, but the visual of Rex's half stump dick sent me over the top. Rex glared at me, "You and this motherfucker . . ." he said as he pointed at Fred. "He attacked me and you shot me. My whole focus in life has been to get my revenge, and I succeeded." I watched as he wickedly smiled as he limped over to a chair and took a seat like he didn't have a care in the world. "You've been locked up in here for twenty-three-years all because of me. How does that feel?" he laughed. "You asshole," I gritted as I moved towards him. He held his cane out towards me. "You better watch it or these boys over here will give you a little shot," he laughed again. The attendants stood in the corner, ready to step in when needed. "Ocean, please take a seat next to your mother," Dr. Green spoke up again, "Mr. Alvarez you as well, please." My mother and I both made our way to our seats. She just kept shaking her head as she then said, "I can't believe this shit." Fred reluctantly took a seat next to my mother. I did not take my eyes off of Rex or Fred. I couldn't decide who I wanted to kill more. "Ocean, it's nice to finally meet you," Dr. Green stated. I smirked, "You are the reason for this bullshit. No one ever had to know any of this bullshit. Everything was fine the way it was." "No, Ocean, it was not. You did not have to take all of the pain. You deserved a chance too." "It was fine!" I shouted, "That's why I'm here!" "But, Ocean, you have done some things that have caused pain as well," Dr. Green said. "Yeah, this bitch shot me!" Rex shouted. "Is that true?" Fred asked. I nodded and laughed, "Yeah, I shot that black bastard. Do you know what he did to Moneca? She really loved him and the motherfucker was using her the whole time. He tried to groom her to become one of his hoes. He had her gang raped and he made a profit off of it. Can you believe that shit? Then, to top it off, when she showed up to his apartment, this motherfucker beat her ass like she was a grown ass man." Rex clapped his hands. "I sure did because I'm a motherfucking pimp! You knew what you were getting into and don't no bitch come up in my house putting their hands on me!" "Oh, but this nigga Fred whooped your ass!" I spat. "Don't matter," he said, "I still got the last laugh." "All this time, I thought Rex was doing this to us because of what I did," Fred shook his head in confusion, "But, it was because you shot him?" "My revenge was towards you as well, Fred. But, I had a special hate in my heart for her. I ripped away her chances of ever having a real life. She never got a chance to see her daughter grow up. I didn't know it at the time, I thought it was Moneca that shot me, but it was you, Ocean, or whatever you call yourself. It doesn't matter though, because you're one in the same. I got my revenge. I had all the power, all because this mother fucker was afraid to go to jail," he pointed at Fred. "I would have done anything for Oneca" Fred said, hitting hit chest. I jumped out of my chair, "Are you fucking serious? You molested Oneca for years!" "Say what?" Rex and my mother exclaimed. "Yeah, despite the fact that Rex tried to set him up. Fred is, in fact, a child molester." "Is this true?" Dr. Green asked Fred. Even the attendants were leaning forward awaiting his response. Fred, once again hung his head in shame, "I never touched Oneca, it was always Ocean." he stated. My mother reached back and slapped the shit out of him. I swear I thought I seen his mustache fly across the room. "Wynita! You can't become physically violent!" Dr. Green exclaimed. "Now, you see why I want to fuck him up!" I said to Dr. Green At this point, Dr. Green had pretty much lost control over the entire situation. The two male attendants stepped closer to my mother, but did not touch her. Fred's hand covered his face where my mother had hit him, and he continued to hold his head down in shame as he then said, "I was able to tell at an early age that there was another side to Oneca. Eventually, that other side began to appear more often and she told me her name. It was Ocean. Temptations that I tried to fight for years, eventually took over, and yes I began a relationship with Ocean." "A relationship? Motherfucker are you crazy? She was a little girl!" I screamed. "Yes, Oneca was a little girl, but you Ocean, you are not." " What the fuck?" Rex said in complete shock. "Ocean, do you mean to tell us, that both Moneca and Oneca developed you as an alternative identity?" Dr. Green asked in disbelief. "Yes, the same identity," I stated, "Their bond was that tight."

"Remarkable," Dr. Green stated, as he jotted quick notes. "Motherfucker, you're going to jail," my mother yelled at Fred as she took out her cell phone. A loud commotion coming from outside instantly caused us to stop fussing at each other and to look at Dr. Green's office door. It sounded as if someone was attempting to force their way in. I felt extremely weak and exhausted. Maybe Dr. Green was right, maybe it was a good thing for all of Moneca's past to be revealed to her. I felt like a heavy weight had been lifted from my shoulders. I felt like I could finally let my guard down.

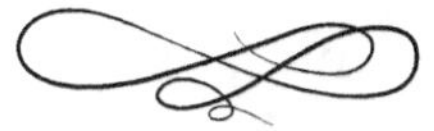

Chapter 18

ONECA

I had to force my way into my mother's doctor's office. Mikey and I were denied entry into the psychiatric facility, but we had found a way to sneak in through the cafeteria's loading dock. I knew we had to move quickly, so I stopped a patient walking down the hallway and asked her where we could find Moneca Alvarez. She said her name was Kina and she led us to a Dr. Green's office. His secretary attempted to stop us, but I was a woman on a mission and nothing was going to keep me from my mother anymore. After I stormed out of the police station, I felt so helpless. The information that my father told me was too much for me. I just couldn't believe that he was telling me that I had multiple personalities. I went straight to my apartment so that I could process my thoughts. In reality, it did answer many of the questions that I had most of my life. The unexplained events and the various people claiming I did things that I had no recollection of, it all made complete sense. Apparently, Mikey followed me home because shortly after he was knocking on my door. "Oneca, come on! Please, open the door," he begged as he knocked on my front door. I was so angry at Mikey, I didn't even want to look at him. "Go away, Mikey!" I yelled through the door. "Oneca, please! I need to talk to you. It's important." "Mikey, you're a liar!" "Oneca, I never lied to you! I tried to help you!" he pleaded. I snatched the door open out of anger. "How did you know Mikey? How did you know that I wa . . .that I was . . ." I was at a loss for words. Mikey walked into my apartment and said, "Oneca, just hear me out, okay?" I nodded as I watched him shut the door. "First of all, you got to know that I love you," his random words threw me for a loop. "Mikey, I . . ."I paused, not knowing what to say. "Just hold on," he cut me off. "Oneca, I have to make a confession and I just hope that you can forgive me because I really do love you and you mean the world to me." "What is it?" I asked. I watched him take a deep breath, he fidgeted for a second and then he came over to me, took my hand, and led me to the couch. Mikey and I both sat down on the couch. I stared into his eyes with concern I had never seen Mikey like this. "Oneca, my father used to be a pimp. He has lived in a few different places, but he knew your parents when he lived in Oklahoma." "Mikey, what are you talking about?" I asked as I snatched my hand away from him, but he grabbed it again and held it in his hands. "My mother's name is Mona and she was one of his main girls. My father's name is Rex. He and your mother had a relationship when she was younger. Some pretty bad things happened to your mother while she was involved with my father. She retaliated by shooting him. He was never the same after that. He has spent the last two decades with revenge in his heart." I looked at him with disgust as I snatched my hand away from his, again. "Mikey, what the hell?" I shrieked. "I know it sounds crazy, but just let me finish. My dad has never been a good man. He was bad to my mom and I. He used to beat the both of us. I was basically an abused and neglected child. He hated the fact that I was nothing like him. I never had an interest in drugs and pimping women. Despite the fact that he was a bad father, I still felt like I would do anything just to earn his approval. Years ago, he sent me here to befriend you. He wanted me to keep any eye on you and initially that's what I did. I don't know exactly what my father had planned for your family because he always kept me in the dark. All he asked was that I check in with him and update him on you. I didn't mean to, but I fell in love with you, Oneca. You had to have sensed it. When you first came to me about the things that had been happening to you, I just wanted to do whatever I could to help." "This is all too much," I shook my head. "One night, I came to your home to talk to you and I saw City leaving your place. I was upset that you lied to me about knowing him that day at the deli, but most of all, I was jealous. When I knocked on your door, you opened the door half naked, with a devious look in your eye. But I didn't care, I started going off about how you lied. You invited me in and listened to everything that I had to say. I basically confessed my love for you and you told me that you loved me, too. We made love that night and I thought everything was finally working out for the both of us. The next day, you acted like nothing ever happened. We met for lunch and you didn't mention anything about our previous night together. I wasn't sure if I should bring it up or not. I quickly figured out that you weren't yourself. The next night, when I showed up at your apartment again, I met your other identity, and she is the complete opposite of you. I immediately knew something wasn't right. She admitted that it was her the whole time I was with you the previous night and you knew nothing about how I felt. She said that City was actually involved with her and that there was nothing I could do about it because if I ever tried to tell you then she would just take over and force you into oblivion. I didn't know what to do. I even tried to pay City to leave you alone, but he took my money and never left you alone. I finally came up with the plan to hire Nate. I figured after time he would discover what was going on and he would reveal it to you.""Nate showed me pictures of you leaving my place late one night. He also had pictures of City. I also saw you giving city a package one day outside of your job," I said as all the pieces began to fall together. "It was just that one time, Oneca, I swear. I just wanted him to leave you alone. We did have sex, but it wasn't you, I thought it was you. I know you may not want to trust me because of what I have told you, but I swear I don't care what my father says or does, I just want to protect you. I just want to be with you." "Mikey, I don't know," I sighed. "Please, just give me a chance to help you," he pleaded. "I don't think there's anything else that can be done for me," I said with sadness in my voice. "Yes, actually, there is. Your mother is still out there. We can go to her." My eyes lit up "You would go with me?" He nodded and said, "I overheard your father on his cell phone stating that he was on his way to Texas. I think he was headed to where she is. I have a feeling something's getting ready to go down. When I tried to call my father, he told me he was on his way to Texas too. "I need to be there," I said. So after that happened, Mikey and I left for Texas the first thing that next morning. By the time we were able to force ourselves into Dr. Green's office, pandemonium had already erupted. As soon as we passed through the door, everyone's eyes went to us. "Oneca!" the familiar looking lady shouted my name and ran to me as fast as she could. "My baby," she cried as she wrapped her arms around me, "It's me baby, it's me; your mother!" I could barely understand her as she cried so hard that snot and tears mixed as they glided down her face. When reality finally hit me, my leaky faucets were flowing non-stop as well. "Mommy," I cried, hugging her back. Another woman came and wrapped her arms around the both of us. "I'm your grandma, baby." "Well, ain't this about a bitch," I heard the dark skinned man who was leaning on a walking cane say. I recognized him from Nate's pictures, "Mikey, what the fuck are you doing here? Did you bring her here?" he asked. "Yes, I did," Mikey stepped up and said. "Mikey, you know Rex?" My father asked. He had been sitting in a chair on the other side of my grandma. "Rex is my father, Mr. Alvarez." "That's right," Rex laughed, "Mikey, you just wait until we get out of here. I swear you aren't good for anything just like your sorry ass whore of a mother. I swear, you can't be my real son, I wouldn't believe it I hadn't seen the DNA results. What did I do to deserve a weak ass son like you?" Mikey held his head down as his father belittled him. I felt so sorry for him. "Your daddy is going to pay for what he did to you," My mother said. "Because he kept us apart?" I asked. "No, baby," My mommy said, "He was wrong for that too, but he was being controlled by this sorry excuse of a man," she motioned her hand towards Rex. "But, your father is going to pay because he has been molesting you since you were a little girl." My eyes widened in horror as years and year of memories of sexual abuse began to rewind and fast forward in my mind. Images of my daddy coming into my bedroom, him climbing on top of me, him putting his mouth on me; they were all so vivid. I saw him inserting his penis into me, grinding on top of me, caressing me, making me do things to him. The memories were too much and I couldn't mentally accept them as they replayed over and over again. I tried to grab onto my mother for support but suddenly, everything in the room went black.

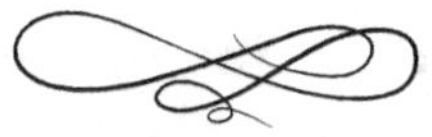

Chapter 19

ONECA
TWO YEARS LATER ...

"Oneca, baby, hurry up!" I could hear Mikey calling my name as I tried to hurry and put my earrings on. He had a special romantic evening planned for us as we were celebrating our two year anniversary. It's been two years of pure bliss. Mikey is my everything and the first man I've ever loved. The road to our happiness was definitely a bumpy journey, but we made it and we were standing strong together. I selected a tight fitting black dress to wear for our special evening. It hugged my curves just perfectly and I knew Mikey would love it. There was no doubt in my mind that Mikey was planning on proposing this evening at dinner. I wanted to look perfect. I stood in the mirror admiring myself and making sure that everything was in place. I could hear the phone ring and Mikey reluctantly answering it. I smiled to myself as I thought about how much I just loved that man. He had been by my side through some of my toughest moments and I knew he was the one for me. My life has changed drastically since that day in Dr. Green's office. I fainted after the suppressed memories of my father molesting me emerged. The memories were just too much for me to bear. Since then, my father was indeed charged and convicted of child molestation and is currently serving fifteen years in prison. I did testify against him in court and I was pleased with the sentence that was handed to him. All charges for fraud and embezzlement against me were dropped. I have maintained my treatment for the past two years, too. I attend weekly counseling sessions and faithfully take my psychotropic medications. According to those closest to me, Ocean has not appeared in a very long time. My mother was released from the psychiatric facility and is doing well. We all moved back to Oklahoma City to have a fresh start. My mother has been readjusting to life in the real world and has enjoyed every moment of getting to know me. It amazes me that even though we were separated from each other when I was just two years old, we still held such a strong bond. Dr. Green said that the fact that we both developed the same alternative identity was unbelievable and a miracle within itself. My mother is working at a local bakery and is living on her own in a nice one bedroom apartment not too far from Mikey and I. Mikey is still working in banking and I have taken a complete career change and have been working as a page operator for the local hospital. Rex was never charged for any crimes. Amazingly, out of all the havoc he caused, he never broke any laws. Unfortunately, he was able to walk away from Dr. Green's office that day without a worry in the world. Disgustingly, my grandmother Wynita ultimately decided to remain married to him. She stated that although she did not agree with what he did, she understood his reasoning and could understand how someone could get so wrapped up into seeking revenge. She owed her sanity to him and refused to leave him. My mother and I have not spoken to her in over a year. If she can't see that she was just a pawn in his game, then maybe she deserves to be with him. Especially after he single handedly was the cause for me being ripped away from my mother and her being locked away for twenty-three-years. "Oneca, grab the phone baby!" Mikey called out to me. "Hello?" I said into the bedroom telephone. "Hi, baby," I could hear my mother smiling through the phone. She was always so happy now. "Hey, Mom. Mikey and I are on our way out the door to dinner." "I know, honey.

I just wanted to invite you guys over to dinner tomorrow evening." "That will be nice, would you like us to bring anything?" "Just that nice shiny new ring that you may get tonight," she laughed. I laughed along with her. I had already confided in her that I thought Mikey would be proposing tonight. "Okay, Mom. We will see you tomorrow." I hung up the phone and grabbed my purse as I headed into the living room. "I'm coming, baby." "Wow baby," he said, admiring me as I walked towards him. "You look beautiful. I'm so lucky to have you." Just then, the phone rang interrupting us yet again. "Hello?" I said quickly pulling the phone to my ear. "O- baby, What's up, my love?" a deep familiar voice boomed through the phone, causing me to freeze. It couldn't be, no it just couldn't be. "Hello?" I said again, as if I hadn't just heard the familiar voice. "Ocean, it's me baby your long lost love, City. I have missed you." "How did you get this number? Don't call here anymore." "Baby, you can't get rid of me that easily." "You're crazy!" "Look, I know all about how your identities are split, but you can't hold my baby Ocean down!" "Ocean doesn't exist!" I yelled into the phone. By this time Mikey had rushed to my side. "Give me the phone," Mikey demanded, but I ignored him. "Is that my boy Mikey?" City laughed, "Tell that nigga I said what up?" "What do you want?" I asked. "Tell that man of yours that he better give you a long kiss goodbye because my baby's coming back for good if I have anything to do with it. I love her and she loves me and we're going to be together. I get out soon and I'm coming for you! You hear me Ocean?!" he yelled into the phone like a lunatic, "I'm coming for you soon be strong for Daddy !!!!!!!!!

TO BE CONTINUED

All Kinds of
CRAZY

2

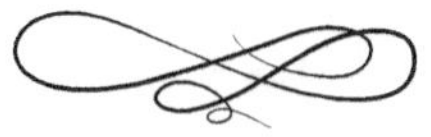

Chapter 1

MIKEY

Women ain't shit. I'm tired of being the good guy. All my life I've had to take shit from other people. It all started from my father. I've had to listen to him tell me over and over about how I'm weak, powerless, frail, and won't ever amount to anything. And what do I do while he's castigating my balls? Not a damn thing! Just sit there and let him talk to me like I'm a punk. Well I, Michael Jarrod Lee, am tired of being disrespected. I've let my father, Raymond Lee aka Rex, berate me my whole life and I'll be damned if I let a woman make me feel like less of a man. I know Oneca is cheating on me. I can feel it in my gut. I just haven't been able to prove it. She just don't act the same. I'm tired of everyone thinking that I'm some kind of punk. I'm sick of being walked over. I know Oneca has problems but I never thought that she would do me wrong, especially after everything that I've been through with her. I'm so in love with the beautiful, Oneca Cheyenne Alvarez. This is the woman who I got down on one knee and asked to be my wife. The only woman I've ever loved, other than my mama of course. I would give Oneca the world, but something's not right. Yes, she went through some crazy things in her life. Yes, she learned that she had another identity, the infamous Ocean, but I didn't and still don't care. I was sent into Oneca's life under false pretenses by my father, but quickly fell in love with her beauty and innocence. It killed me every day to not be able to tell her how I really felt and that my father was obsessed with her family. I've never been anything like my father. I had no interest in pimping women or selling drugs. I'm just a low key type of guy who likes watching sports and anything that has to do with science fiction. Some might consider me a square, but I am who I am, and I've been okay with that for years. When I first saw Oneca, I couldn't believe how beautiful she was. When she looked at me with those slanted, brown eyes, I felt like the world stood still. In my eyes, she was so pure and she liked me for me. Each day that our friendship grew, I felt horrible for deceiving her, but I was slowly falling for her, and felt like I would never get the chance to tell her. After all that Oneca went through in her life, and learning of all the people who betrayed her, she still chose to keep me around. She loved me all along, just like I had loved her, and I was grateful for that. We'd been going strong for two years and I planned on asking her to be my wife. A phone call from Ocean's boyfriend, City, ruined everything. It was times like that, I wished that I had the ruthless heart of my father because if I could kill City I would have. I didn't understand why he couldn't leave her alone, I mean he was in prison for a reason, and she put him there. As far as I know, Ocean has not returned. All of the horrible events from Oneca and Moneca's past have been revealed, and they are both learning to cope with these things through therapy. Ocean was created to protect them from the terrible things that they experienced because they were not able to mentally handle them. But now that all of these things from their past have been presented to them, the need for a protector does not exist. If City is ever successful in bringing Ocean back, then I could lose Oneca forever. I have laid next to her at night, and I've heard her mention his name. I've never told her this, but I know she dreams about him. I can tell that she doesn't fear him either, it's almost like she longs for him. She won't let me make love to her but she moans in her sleep like she's giving it him. It pisses me off that she's with me and she's dreaming about this dude. I can't get the thoughts out of my mind of Oneca cheating on me. I proposed to Oneca and she accepted, but she won't pick a wedding date and I feel that she has been procrastinating. She claims that she would like to take time to get herself together and make sure that she is really okay. But I just don't know if I buy it. Oneca, her mother, and I all moved to Oklahoma City to start over. I was able to get a job with the Bank of Oklahoma and maintain my career as an account specialist. Oneca took a job at the OU Children's Hospital as an operator and eventually decided that she would like to go back to school and earn a degree in Nursing. This has taken up so much of her time and I'm starting to feel like a second thought to her. Between her attending school, her therapy sessions, and still working as an operator at night, I don't feel like I ever get to see my fiancée. I've tried to stay cool about it, but I have developed obsessive thoughts about Oneca being with another man. She doesn't know it, but three weeks ago I downloaded an application to her cell phone that allows me to track all of her whereabouts. I spy on her all the time. I follow her around and I'm just waiting on the day when I catch her ass up. I hadn't noticed anything odd about her whereabouts until today. I didn't know what the hell she was doing on the West side of the city, but this was not the first time that I'd tracked her there. I knew her classes were over for the day, but normally she would go straight home to prepare for work that night.

She attended class at the University of Oklahoma in Norman which was about 20 miles south of OKC. We lived on the North side right off of Memorial road, so what the hell was she doing way out on 122nd and Council? After some time had passed I noticed that she had been at this same location for over an hour. I didn't know who the hell lived there, but my pride couldn't take it anymore. I needed to find out what was going on. I quickly made up an excuse to leave work and drove straight to the residential area.

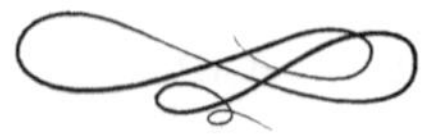

Chapter 2

MIKEY

When I arrived I noticed her black Acura parked in the driveway along with another white SUV. I knew she was messing around on me, I could feel it. I parked down the street from the brick home making sure that I could get a good view of what was going on. I had not thought this plan out entirely as I was unsure of what to do now. I watched the home for about an hour. I called her cell phone several times and it pissed me off each time that she didn't answer. I texted her, 'Hey Babe Call me', but she didn't still didn't respond. Although I wanted to, I knew deep down that I didn't have the balls to go up to that house and confront her. Just as I was getting ready to drive away, my ringing phone startled me. "Hello?" "Is this my traitor ass son?" "What do you want pops?" I responded in an exasperated tone. "What you doing?" He asked. "Why?" I was short with him. "Damn, son! Why so hostile?" He laughed. I let out a deep breath out of frustration, "You only call when you want something, so what is it?" "Tell your crack head ass mama to stay away from my house. My wife and I are getting tired of her shit," "For real Pops? That's how you feel? It's your fault she's even strung out in the first place," "Blame who you want. You just need to get her in check. Tell her to quit coming around here begging, I aint got shit for her. And who the hell you think you talking to anyway? Nigga, I'm still your daddy," I shook my head out of frustration. If he would have stayed in Georgia, he wouldn't have to worry about my mama. "Look, I got to go," "What you doing? Worrying about that psycho ass woman of yours?" "I already told you not to ever mention Oneca again," I said. "Oh nigga, just because you got your feelings hurt the last time, don't mean I'm not gone tell it how it is. I told you she wasn't shit, but you aint shit either, so I guess it's a match made in heaven. But since you do have my blood running through you, I at least got a little sympathy for your dumb ass, so I try to offer a little advice. You think that bitch aint fucking around? She's a hoe, just like her mama," he laughed into the phone, "It runs in their family," "Oh yea, but you are the one who is married to her grandma? What kind of shit is that?" "Don't worry about what the fuck I do. Just know this; I'm always 2 steps ahead. Never underestimate

Rex Lee," he laughed at himself. "Yea whatever, like I said, I'm busy," I said with disgust. "Hey watch your tone young man," he said mockingly, "Just remember what your pops told you, you'll thank me one day. I guarantee, my words will ring true," I couldn't stand the sound of his cackling for one more second, "Don't forget what I said about your mama." He said before hanging up. I wonder what God was trying to prove by giving me the life that I'd been given. Why did Rex have to be my father? Why did I have to son of a drug addicted whore and a self-centered ass pimp? The only thing that did make sense in my life was my love for Oneca, and hell, her parents were just as fucked up as mine. Movement down the street caused me to refocus my attention. I saw a tall thin Hispanic girl come out of the house. I recognized her as Oneca's friend, Camilla. I breathed a sigh of relief as I realized that I was overreacting again. My phone suddenly went off alerting me that I had a text, 'Hey baby had to stay late at class, just now headed home. Love you.' I read Oneca's lying ass text. I threw the phone on the floor of my car out of frustration, wondering why in the hell she was lying. I suddenly noticed a man exit the home followed by Oneca. I tried to study the guy from so far away. He was light skinned, tall, about 6'4", with a scruffy goatee. He had a little weight on him from what I could tell, as they were all dressed in scrubs. My baby was just smiling from ear to ear and laughing with the both of them. I watched her give the Latina girl a hug and her and the guy jumped in her car. I ducked down in my seat praying to God that she drove the other direction. After a few moments I raised in my seat. What the fuck was this nigga doing in her car? "Damn Oneca, you fucking around on me?" I said out loud to myself. "I told your dumb ass!" I heard a muffled voice exclaim. I looked around confused, then noticed my phone on the floor where I had thrown it. I picked it up noticing that my pops was still on the phone. Damn did my phone accidentally dial him? I put the phone to my ear, not knowing what to say, I felt humiliated. "I know you on here," he stated, "When you gone learn son? Daddy knows best." I hung up the phone pissed at the world.

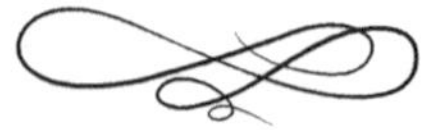

Chapter 3

ONECA

I glanced over at Rashaad as we rode down the highway. He sure was handsome, but nothing could compare to my baby Mikey. I couldn't wait to get home and spend a little time with him before my night shift at the hospital. Life has been going pretty well for me. I just wish Mikey wouldn't act so crazy and jealous. Ever since City called our home, my man has not been the same. I don't know what I can do to convince him that I don't want anyone, but his ass. It's becoming stressful because he is always accusing me of something. He has started making me feel constrained, like I can't be free to do what I want. He treats me exactly like my father used to treat me. He has never said it, but I think he believes that Ocean may come back around and leave a trail of destruction like she has in the past. I'm scared to tell Mikey that there are times that I still black out because I'm scared might leave me. There are times when I have missed big chunks of my days and I don't who I've been with or where I been. Everyone around me acts as if nothing is happening, so I try to act as normal as possible. But the black outs have been getting worse and worse. Working at the Children's Hospital as an operator, did cause me to gain an interest in nursing, so I made the decision to enter Nursing school a year ago. It has been going really well. I get along with all of my classmates, but I've become really close with Camilla and Rashaad. We all could relate to each other because we all wanted to go into Pediatric Nursing. Camilla's personality was the opposite of mine, she was a fireball. Her outgoing personality and beauty caused her to constantly be the center of attention. She was thin, but shapely and her beautiful dark hair flowed down her back. She did not have a Mexican accent, but would curse you out in Spanish at the drop of a dime. Rashaad was tall and handsome. He was definitely a pretty boy with his light brown skin and curly dark hair. He actually was a top Basketball player at the University of Oklahoma, but 6 years ago a leg injury caused him to have to hang up his dreams of entering the NBA. He dropped out of school for a while, but finally decided to re-enroll at OU as a nursing student. He was definitely the class clown and was always cracking jokes. Although I'd never seen him in action, I also believed him to be a ladies man. "Oneeeca….earth to Oneca," Rashaad waved his hand in front of my face, snapping me out of my thoughts. "Oh, my bad," I said smiling. "Damn girl," he laughed, "I need you to pay attention while you driving me around, I would like to live to see 26," he joked. "Boy please, you will get home safely," I teased. "Take this next exit," he said pointing up ahead, "I appreciate you giving me a ride home, my truck should be out of the shop tomorrow," "No problem, I'm just glad we were able to get some more study time in. That test next week is going to be a beast," I sighed. "I know man, got a nigga rethinking this whole nursing thing," he said as he directed me into his apartment complex off of NW Expressway and Macarthur. "Rashaad, you make the best grades in the class, don't play," "I know, I do, don't I?" He said rubbing his goatee in a cocky way. "Boy get out of my car," I laughed while parking in an open space. "Yea, we wouldn't want your man to come jumping out the bushes," he joked. I smiled, although I know Rashaad was only joking, he just didn't know how crazy Mikey had been acting lately. "Aww shit. Did I hit a nerve?" he asked noticing that I didn't laugh at his joke. "Naw, me and my boo are good," I replied quickly. "As good as you look, I would hide in the bushes any day." he laughed opening the door and getting out. I didn't know what to say, he had never complimented me like that before. I watched him unlock his door and turn around and wave to me. I didn't want to let Rashaad know, but his joke had hit a nerve. I didn't think Mikey was bold enough to hide in bushes, but he definitely would not have liked the fact that I gave Rashaad a ride home. Lately, he didn't like anything that I did that didn't involve him. That's why I lied and told him I had to stay at school late. A couple of weeks ago Camilla and I went and got something to eat after class. Mikey lost his damn mind when I didn't show up at home at my usual time. He started flipping out and accusing me of cheating on him. I hate lying to him, but it was just easier that way. He is just so insecure and I can't stand it. I try to cut him some slack because I know he catches a lot of hell from his father for being with me. His father hates my family, which is ironic because we should have a hit out on him for all the bullshit he has put my family through. I wish Mikey would learn how to stand up to his father. I can't stand to see him and his father interact with each other. Mikey resorts to being this meek little boy and his father is an asshole. To add even more drama to the mix, my grandmother, Wynita, is married to Mikey's father Rex. My mother, Moneca, and I haven't spoken to her in a long time because she decided to stay married to Rex even after she learned all of the horrible things he did to my mother. How in the hell can you stay married to a man who used to be with your daughter in the first place? On top of that he had her raped, beat the shit out of her, raped again, and then was the reason behind her being held in a psychiatric facility against her will. I know my grandma didn't have the easiest life either, but that's no excuse. According to my mother, when her husband left her she completely lost it. She went into some sort of depressive lethargic state for years. My mother thinks that losing another man would probably kill her so she tries not to take it personal. I, personally, take it really personal. You would think I would let family betrayal roll off my back. A little over two years ago I learned that my father, well the man that raised me, sexually abused me as a child. His excuse was that it wasn't me, but only Ocean during all of the intimate encounters. My other identity, Ocean, did in fact protect me during the abuse, and I was never aware of what was going on. This man raised me by himself and I adored him. Growing up without a mother, I did have moments where I felt incomplete, but my father was able to make me feel more than loved. When the abuse was revealed, it was too much for me to handle. It took some time for me to be able to process what was being told to me. Dr. Green recommended, Dr. Barnett, a psychiatrist here in Oklahoma City that I could see on a weekly basis. Dr. Barnett is great and has really helped me work through the memories of abuse that sporadically come to me. It all started to make sense on why I was never comfortable with my sexuality, and even to this day, I have not been able to make love with Mikey. I was forced to make a hard decision when I had to testify against my father and he was ultimately sentenced to 20 years in prison. I haven't seen or heard from him since. I wondered if Mikey was even home as I pulled into our apartment complex because I did not see his car. I parked and grabbed my things hurrying inside. The house was dark as I walked in. I walked into the bedroom and screamed out as I noticed a dark figure sitting on the bed. I ran back to the door, "Get your ass up!" I yelled to the intruder as I grabbed a knife off the kitchen bar. The figure did not move, but just sat there looking at me. Confused I flipped on the bedroom light. "Mikey! What the hell are you doing! Why are you playing? Sitting in here in the dark," "Why did you do it?" He said in a low voice. "Do what? What is wrong with you?" I exclaimed. "You fucking around on me? Is that why you won't let me make love to you?" He accused. "Mikey are you serious?" "Just answer the damn question!" His voice rose, but he remained on the bed. "Mikey, baby I don't know what you are talking about," I said moving closer to him. I was shocked to see that his eyes were bloodshot, "Baby have you been drinking?" my question was immediately answered as I caught a whiff of the alcohol on his breath. "Hell yea I've been drinking," he spit, "My fiancée is a fucking whore," I was so taken aback by his words that I was speechless. "You aint shit," he glared at me. "Why are you talking to me like that?" I could feel the tears on the rims of my eyelids. "Why don't you ask that nigga you were with today?" It suddenly hit me, he must have seen me with Rashaad today, "Baby it's not what you think, I swear. Rashaad is in my study group," "I don't give a damn," he yelled, quickly standing up, "You nothing, but a slut just like your damn mama!" "What!" I said out of shock. Mikey had never spoken to me like this before. "You heard me," he spit. "Mikey how could you say that about my mother? You know what happened to her?" by now the tears were flowing. "Your mama was a hoe way before that, Oneca, don't try to flip this around. I saw your ass with him today," "I just gave him a ride! His truck is in the shop! We were at Camilla's studying," I exclaimed. "And to think, I wanted you to be my wife," he turned his nose up as he stumbled into the bathroom. By now, I was furious. I quickly took the ring off throwing it at the back of his head, "Take your ring! You asshole! I can't believe you talking to me like that," "Take your ass out of here," he yelled. "Oh, I'm going to work, you bastard!" I slammed the door as I left our apartment.

MY BROTHER'S
KEEPER

BOOK II

Chapter 1
HELP WANTED -KANE-

On the ride back to the apartment. I was trying to conceive what just happened at the warehouse. The Planner sent a trained killer. Smoke and I didn't speak. He probably thought about his share of the money. At this point, we could only imagine that much cash. Everything we had planned was now ruined. I have a diamond worth millions and don't know who else to sell it to. I don't have another buyer. I thought about the bank robbery and the heist. The two crimes I committed after being framed for murder. Trouble seems to follow me around now. I thought for certain things would get better after I sold the rock to The Planner. That's far from happening now. I should have expected a guy like that would try to kill me. The only option I have is to wait for him to call. The thought of putting myself in danger a second time is a shame. I'm asking to die. I adjusted the seat to a more relaxing position and took a deep breath. I don't have a million questions like some people. I only need the answer to one. If somebody can answer me out there in a world people take for granted. I would greatly appreciate it. I didn't expect my life to turn out this way, I was good. I had the best family anyone could ever ask for. Things changed and everything suddenly went south. Why? That's the only question I need someone to answer. Why? The question behind every remark. A simple word that seems to be more of a comeback question. I wonder what my friends would want to know? Smoke would ask about his grandmother. Why did she have to die at sixty-five? Redd, why didn't he have a stronger leg? People recover from leg injuries, but he didn't. Bear would want to know why he had to be the one with a sleeping disorder. He could have been an amazing football player. Kim would ask about not receiving a track scholarship. She was one of the top runners in the state at the time. Many things in life are left unexplained. You just have to take the road that was chosen for you without question. I took the diamond out of my pouch and gave it a mean stare. I turned it side to side. I came close to death two times for this fucking rock. The value of this thing is life-threatening. What the hell was I thinking of when I decided to steal it in the first place? I saw Smoke glance at it. "What do you think we should do?" I broke the silence without looking at him. My attention was on the death rock. "About what?" He asked in a calm voice. "Everything," I whispered. "Starting with this. What do you suggest we do with this damn thing? This… this shit is getting crazy. I mean… what I'm trying to say is… I never pictured us as criminals. Man… we have been best friends since high school. We're supposed to be living it up right now. Running, balling, football, whatever." I felt my emotions taking over. "We were good at everything. The best and nobody could touch us. How can something so good turn out this damn bad?" I felt my blood simmering. Smoke was silent. Maybe he was remembering those moments in high school when we blew out our competition. Somebody is about to get smoked. Two high school state titles in track. That's what the phrase meant. Man… those were the days. Look at the person I've become since then. My father would disown me for what I've done. And he's the one who told me to take care of my mother by any means necessary. The car pulled into the apartments. I was ready to get out when Smoke spoke up. "Kane, we do what we have to do. You're smarter than you think. I trusted you with the bank and the museum heist. Call me insane, but I didn't do it because you're my friend. I did it because I believe in you." He smiled. I closed my fist and gave my best friend some dap. I needed that. I went into the apartment feeling better. Kim wasn't home. I was exhausted from everything that happened today. I walked directly to the bedroom and crashed on the bed. Now I know how tired you can get from a gun battle.

Chapter 2
WAKE UP CALL

"How do I catch the ball?" I asked. "It's bigger than me." My father walked over and showed me how to spread my fingers. He was teaching me how to catch a football. "Keep your finger's apart son and when the ball comes in your direction. Wrap your hands around it, ok?" I held my hands out with my fingers spread just like he told me. "But… I'm scared." He walked about ten yards away from me. I followed close behind and made it two yards before he told me to stop. He said I'm supposed to be a few feet away. I had to stay put and catch an enormous ball. "There's no reason to be scared, son. The ball won't hurt you." I held my hands out while still trying to follow my father. The helmet felt too big for my head. My skull felt heavier than before. I couldn't see straight with it covering my eyes. I wanted to take it off. I felt a sudden sting in my stomach. "Ouch!" He had thrown the ball and it hit me in the center of my chest. I wasn't ready for it and I started to cry. I left the ball on the ground and walked in his direction. When I made it to him, the air in my three-year-old chest slowly returned. He ran in the opposite direction towards the ball. The oversized helmet caused me to walk off-balance. My hands were in a catch position as I followed behind him. The blow to my chest brought tears to my eyes. I didn't like the football game we were playing. I wanted to stop. I felt the ball hit my hands. It stung a little, but not like the first time. I continued forward with my hands out and tripped face forward over the ball. "Ouch." My hands hit the ground. The helmet felt like a block of stone and I collapsed on the ground. Grass and dirt got in my mouth. It was hard to get up. I thought my father was walking over to pick me up. Instead, he grabbed the football and ran in the opposite direction. Somewhere, the distinct sound of my brother laughing could be heard. His voice was clear and not inspiring. I got up from the ground and noticed my father standing in the distance. For some reason, my hands were out with my fingers spread apart. I walked towards him. "I hate foo…" I felt a sting in my hands. The world around me became silent. The sound of my brother laughing, couldn't be heard anymore. I was no longer crying as I continued walking towards my father, ready to end my football career in three catch attempts. I opened my eyes to see if he was in front of me. Surprisingly, I saw my hands wrapped around the football. I caught it! I approached my father and spiked the ball on the ground. He picked me up and tossed me into the air while cheering. He sounded proud of me. "You caught the ball son! That's my boy." Maybe that was all the inspiration I needed. I caught the football for the first time in my life at the age of three. What a birthday. A loud sound woke me from my dream. I remembered that day vividly. I didn't drop a football again until my sophomore year of high school. Only because I collided with another receiver on the team while going after the ball simultaneously. His fault if you want to know the truth. My side of the field, my route. That was my final season before I got arrested for murder. I looked at the clock, 3:45 am. The alarm sounded. I set the timer when I was searching for a job and forgot to turn it off. I rolled over to get some more rest. Something didn't feel quite right. I checked the time again to assure there was no confusion, 3:46 am. I set up. Strange, I didn't notice this before, Kim was not in the bed.

Chapter 3
MISSING PERSON

My curiosity level rose every second. "Where's Kim?" I felt like a bag of bones. My body, put up a fight as I got out of bed. I had to command my legs to operate. They felt paralyzed. I walked off the numb feeling heading into the living room. I needed some water immediately. My mouth was dry as the Arizona desert. My mind went back to Kim. Perhaps she went out with a friend? That suggestion spent a short amount of time in my mind. No way, she's not the stay out type. Work? Another suggestion that wasn't the right answer. Damn, where could she have gone? I was beginning to seriously worry about her whereabouts. I finished the glass of water. It helped a little. At least my cottonmouth was gone. This had to be how my father felt about my mother. Welcome to stress. There's a possibility she stayed out cheating with another guy. I smiled at that. Perfect time to do it when I gained forty grand in cash and a diamond worth millions. Ok, I shouldn't think about her that way. That was stupid. Damn, I'm getting desperate. I left the kitchen and sat in complete darkness in the living room. If I didn't know any better, I resembled an angry husband, waiting in the middle of the night for his cheating wife to come home. Is this how married people act? Apparently so. My eyes were wide, anticipating her to walk through the door at any moment. What other alternative do I have? Maybe, I should have stayed home. The Planner tried to kill me and now Kim is suddenly missing. I don't know what to think or how to feel. "Shit," I whispered. I thought back to when I switched my phone on vibrate after Smoke and I left the restaurant. How did I forget something like that? What if she tried to call my phone? I hurried to the bedroom. I picked up my pants and grabbed my phone from the left pocket. No, it was dead. I drained the battery. Charger. Where is it? I never misplace it. Now it's gone. Shit. Where did I put that damn thing? I search the entire bedroom with sonic boom speed. I couldn't find it anywhere. Ok, calm down. The living room? I frantically checked the entire area. I felt my heart rate speed up to 200 mph. My adrenaline took over. This could be important. What if something serious happened? I stopped searching to gather my thoughts. I could have a heart attack at the speed I was moving. Think, where was the last place you charged your phone? I didn't, Kim used it. She needs a new one so she borrowed mine. Bedroom, living room, kitchen? She used it in the kitchen. I hurried to the kitchen. Bingo. Right there in front of my face. My charger was plugged into the wall. I connected it to my phone and waited a minute before it gained some power. I had seven missed calls. None were from Kim. What, why? I called her phone five times. Each call ended in her voicemail. I sat on the sofa perplexed. I accidentally turned on the TV by sitting on the remote control. The news turned on. "Oh, my God." Kim's car had been abandoned at the mall. The news headline read, Possible Missing Person.

My Brother's
Keeper

Book III

Chapter 1:
KANE

Touchdown. I dunked the football through the goal post. Champions. I ran to the sideline to look for my father. Everyone was celebrating, making it harder to spot him. I finally found him. He was standing in the middle of a crowd with a dissatisfied look on his face as if he wasn't happy. I stopped ten feet away from him. Something was wrong, so I took off my helmet. A more serious look replaced the smile on my face. I approached him. He didn't say anything, not one word. He looked at me in disgust. "What's wrong?" What came out of my father's mouth shocked me. "Why is Abel still alive?" Suddenly, I heard Kim call my name. My vision became blurry for a second before focusing on the face in front of me. She was just as beautiful as the first day I met her. "You had a bad dream." She looked worried. "It was the same dream as before." "The one about your father?" She sighed. "Yeah," we were home from the hospital. It's been a month and I had this dream five times. I didn't want her to worry about me. She'd been through enough, and I won't let anything happen to her again. I would die for her. "It's ok. You don't have to worry." "Your father wants you to revenge his death. That's why you have bad dreams." She said, concerned. "You guys have been through a lot together. It shouldn't have to be this way. His soul won't rest until Abel is dead." She was right about Abel tormenting my father's soul. We had plenty of father-son moments. That day on the football field, my father congratulated me before we hugged. I remember the day vividly. I caressed the side of her face and smiled. "I know you care, but everything will be ok. I know what I have to do. Not only for my father…you as well." I broke through to her, and she smiled. "I love you, Kane Simmons." "I love you," we kissed passionately. She pulled back and slapped my forehead, playfully. "Get up, and I'll make breakfast." "Slap my forehead again if you want me to kick your butt," I joked. She popped the center of my head. "Do something." "Oh, you want me to do something?" I grabbed her waist and began tickling her. She started laughing uncontrollably and tried to escape my hold. "Ok, I got you." I pulled her closer to my body, working my fingers in every area that would make her cry. "Stop, please stop." She laughed harder and tickled my side, trying to defend herself. "No mas." "That's right," when I released my grip, she slapped my forehead and quickly sprung from the bed. "I'm gonna get you!" I shouted as she ran out of the room. I sighed. "Women." I slowly got up from the bed and stretched my arms and legs. A ray of light shined through the window, and I walked over to open the curtains in my bedroom just enough to see the morning sun. Kim and I have been staying at my house ever since Abel been on the run. My mother had been kidnapped from the hospital, so I control the property until otherwise. There wasn't a reason to worry about my brother showing up unless he wanted to die. I haven't heard anything from him. Every now and then, Smoke or Bear would stay overnight to watch for anything suspicious. We haven't made any moves with the money. Kim was shocked after I told her we have 23 million dollars. Her eyes popped out of her head when I opened the briefcase. I feel much better than before. My stab wound was healing just fine. I give it another week before I'm 90 percent. When I fully recover, I'll search for The Planner. That's the only way to find my mother in time. He wants to trade her for the diamond or the money. He might want both. After I handle that situation, I'll find Abel and put him in the ground so my father's soul can rest. I looked over to my neighbor's backyard and smiled. "My fault, big dawg." The recovery cone around the neck of the dog who attacked me looked like a lamp. I felt sorry for tossing him into a wall, but he was about to kill me. Every time I looked out of the window, he was there waiting for me to show my face to remind me of what I did to him. I shook my head. "You're not the only one who wants me dead." I shut the curtain and got in the shower. After twenty minutes, I made my way downstairs into the kitchen with Kim. The aroma in the air spoke to my stomach. Yeah, I'm hungry. I looked over at her. She was doing her thing while dancing to the music. I stepped behind and grabbed her waist. "Callaloo and shrimp? It smells good." "Thank you," she eased her head under my chin. She looked up, smiled, and kissed my lips. "I'll be back. I need to check on Bear. He fell asleep in my father's office." "He was looking for anything Abel might have left behind." She began mixing the Callaloo." "Bear," I sighed. "I told him I searched it several times and didn't find anything. He's determined to find something. Abel can't hide forever, and the police are after him. I need to find him before then." "Where do you think he's hiding?" She turned down the music. "I don't know," I said honestly. "I have a friend from high school that's helping decode everything in Abel's laptop. Asian kid, Smoke put me in contact with him." "Do you trust him?" "I don't have a choice." I picked up the spatula and tasted the food. "Delicious." "Hey." She slapped my hand. "Ok, I'll be right back." I left the kitchen and walked to the office. The door was left open, and I pushed through. I spotted Bear sleeping in my father's chair with his head down and arms crossed on the desk. "Bear, get up," I shouted as I got closer. To my surprise, it worked. Bear's head shot up from a resting position. "I'm up." He said frantically. I smirked, stunned that it didn't take any effort to wake him. Usually, I had to scream in his ear or shake him. "Kim's cooking Calloloo, it'll be ready soon ." I turned back to the door." "I had a dream." I stopped and turned around. "Me too. I had the same one about my father this morning. Trust me, we all been through hell." "It wasn't like that." He sounded serious. My facial expression changed, and I got a little concerned about the worried look in his eyes. He never before shared with us any of his dreams. The look on his face said the same. What he said next shocked me. "We were searching for Abel in Africa."

Chapter 2:
JORDAN

I drove the car through the woods down a long dirt road. A log cabin came into view. The place appeared deserted on the inside. All of the lights were off, and the driveway leading up to the house was empty. I visited this place every summer when I was younger. It was where my brother and I learned to survive in the wild. My father trained us, and we became skilled hunters by the age of ten and eleven. I haven't spoken to him since I became a cop. It's been years since then. I stopped the car in front of the cabin and turned to Mrs. Simmons. It's been a month, and I thought about killing her every-single-day. She's overly beautiful, but looks are deceiving, and I'm sure she'll slit my throat the first chance she gets. I can't trust anybody, and that's how I like it. Me against the world. "This is the place." Mrs. Simmons glanced around the property. "It doesn't look like anyone is home. If you cannot hold up your end of the deal. I suggest-" "Then I'll kill you." I interrupted. She faced me, and I looked deep into her eyes when I spoke, so she felt the situation›s seriousness. "Remember, you need me. I'm still debating if I should trust you. Wait here, and don't get out of the car. I don't want to put a bullet in your head just yet." I held eye contact with her for a few seconds. She didn't break a sweat at any point in our stare down. I smirked and got out of the car. Don't let your pride get you killed, Mrs. Simmons. I sighed and scanned across the front of the cabin. "Where the fuck are you?" I muttered. Not only can my brother fly a plane, but he is also a master hunter. Just not the kind that hunts animals. That's why we grew apart when I decided to pursue law enforcement. He became a hitman for hire. Flying is a part of the job. At one point in my life, I wanted to bring down bad guys like him. But that all changed when I went undercover in the Mob. Those were the best days of my life. My eyes ran up the pathway to the first step. When dealing with a man who kills for a living, you have to be mindful of booby traps. I cautiously began walking toward the front door, continuing to scan the area as I approached. "Adrian," I called out his name with my hands high to display I wasn't a threat. "Adrian, it's me. Your brother." I tried to peek through the left side window. He had smeared dirt on it. I couldn't see anything on the inside. "Fuck." He's the type of guy who knew you were at the front door. I don't know of anyone who can show up by surprise, and he wasn't aware of their presence. I heard a voice in the distance. "Try the back." I swiftly turned around and spotted Mrs. Simmons standing by the car. "Don't hurt her!" I yelled. Adrian stood behind Mrs. Simmons, ready to attack. I should have known something like this would happen if I brought her along. I'm a fucking idiot. "Ah!" She yelped as my brother grabbed her from behind and put a blade to her throat. "Adrian." I held out my hand, trying to ease any uncertainty about us being here. A surge of anxiety stormed through my blood cells. My mind said, draw your weapon and have some fun. Cat and mouse sound about right. No. Shut the fuck up, Planner! I can't get dirty right now. I have to keep Mrs. Simmons alive if I want the money. Damn, I hate saving people. Lately, I have been thinking as The Planner and agent Jordan. It's as if I'm indecisive about who I want to be. "She has a deal for you, and trust me. You need to hear what she has to say." That wasn't part of the plan, but what the hell. If he kills her, she brought it upon herself. Mrs. Simmons squirmed in my brother's arms before relaxing in his grip. There is nothing she could do to escape. My brother had control of her life. Lucky for her, she wasn't dead yet. Where was the woman I saw in the office? The crying bitch, looking for attention because someone murdered her weapon smuggling husband. She's changing by the second. I'm learning more about her fearless persona as time pass. Keep revealing to me who you really are, Mrs. Simmons. Adrian stood there without moving an inch. His eyes appeared to be black, somewhat vacant. Abel reminded me of my brother. Two lives filled with anger and death. The blade remained pressed against the neck of Mrs. Simmons, sharp enough to cut her head off. Regardless of its size, weapons used by the man in front of me are for fatal blows. Fatality is the only outcome when in war. "I'm not here to arrest you." I stepped off the porch with my hands down by my side. Fuck it. My hands needed to be by my gun. If she dies, she dies. I still have to kill Kane, if anything, for embarrassing me in front of the world. Adrian is deadly, and I had to be ready if he tried to make a move. Deep down, I wanted him to get active. "The woman you're holding can pay you more than double your fee." I stopped approaching midway to keep a safe distance, letting what I said to settle in his mind. "We need you to fly us to Africa. Her dead husband built a smuggling business. He stashed millions of dollars in a safe house, and she's the only person who knows the passcode. That's why I need her. I went out of my way to kidnap her from a mental hospital. Of course, you know I've gone rogue. I made a deal with the Africans, and they think I betrayed them. I wouldn't go there to die. She wants to hire you to fly us there, and if the situation gets dirty, well, you know the deal. This is not a one-man job. After I get my cut, you can fuck off." Suddenly, Mrs. Simmons fell out of his grip and then turned around to face him. "He's telling the truth. I'm the only person who knows the location of the safe. My husband didn't trust anyone to help. He built the safe house with his bare hands. I stood by his side every day until the task was complete. If it's not there, the remainder of my life depends on you." My brother made eye contact with me, then put his attention back on her. "The price is triple, three million."

Chapter 3:
ABEL

I walked out onto the back deck of our family beach house. Jar purchased this as a type of staycation for us five years ago. It's a shame we only came once as a family. That's what you call a father. Spend your hard-earned money where it counts. Kane is a knucklehead. He wouldn't look for me here, although I should not underestimate his intelligence. He found out I murdered our father. Brother vs. brother, I accept the challenge. My focus had to remain on getting the diamond to Africa. That's why I'm here with the rest of my crew. Kane could wait to die at a later date. There is a pilot who goes by the name Silva. His name popped up several times in the black notebook. He used to fly for Jar and made a fortune working for him. The beach house across from ours belongs to him. Who would have thought they were that close? In a matter of seconds, I found all of his information on the internet. I decided to lay low for a while until the heat died down. Only then would it be safe to fly. As of yet, I didn't come across any headlines regarding my name. I used a secure line to hack into the FBI criminal database to clear any warrants for my arrest. What is the use of being a genius if you can't use your intelligence to create an advantage? "Good morning," I heard a lovely voice from behind. I sensed Gina by my side. She leaned on the balcony next to me, close enough to touch. "Good morning to you, beautiful." I meant it. She is not like any other woman I've ever met. Her heart is just as cold as mine, and she's dangerously deceptive to anyone lower than her intellectual level. "You need to speak with Sliva today," Gina spoke in a soft tone. "He hasn't returned since last night." I didn't look at her when I spoke. The morning sun shined across the water, highlighting the breathtaking scenery. The kind of view that could win any woman's heart. "You need to rest." She said. "I'll take over and if he shows himself. I'll wake you, my love." She leaned her head against my shoulder. "Don't worry about me." A year ago, I only thought about taking over the government and becoming the underworld's unquestioned alpha boss. Gina slightly altered my perspective of women. She implements the things Jar used to teach me to be aware of when it came to women. I'm aware of the effects she has on my decision-making. I feel like I have to protect her. I wondered if this was how Kane felt about Kim when he first met her? If so, Gina could stand in the way of a life-time awaited victory. "I won't press the issue." She said. "I think we need to get rid of Bam." The news wasn't shocking. I already knew how she felt about Bam, and I began to feel the same energy. After he left Snake for dead in the hands of an enormous freak of a man, Bam wouldn't survive in Africa. The rebels would tear him apart. I'm intelligent enough to realize she tried to provoke me to perceive that he's weak. "We can't afford to lose a brain that operates as we do. Manpower is crucial at this stage. Cutting him off now won't accelerate anything forthcoming. You need to be patient. His time will come. I promise." She sighed. "It's Silva. His boat is pulling up to the dock." My eyes followed in the direction of Gina's finger. An exotic blue and yellow four-passenger speed boat docked fifty yards away. A skinny, dark-skinned man hopped off the boat with a woman wearing a two-piece bikini. They embraced, and it ended with a kiss before they entered the beach house. The windows were open, and I could see through into the bedroom. I guess he didn't care if anyone was watching, and I've waited all night. I hope he's ready to fly.

ABOUT
THE AUTHOR

New York Times & International Best Selling Author Billie Dureyea Shell was born in Compton California and now lives in Ladera Heights with his wife and kids who he loves to spend time with.

He is the Owner of several properties in the Los Angeles area and gives back to his community by providing low income housing to those who need it. He stated "It doesn't matter where you at or where you from it's what you do with your time. There's nothing you can't do if you put your mind to it".